SPECIAL FORCES CADETS

SPECIAL FORCES CADETS 🦅

RUTHLESS

SPECIAL FORCES CADETS

CHRIS RYAN

SPECIAL FORCES CADETS

RUTHLESS

HOT
KEY
BOOKS

First published in Great Britain in 2020 by
HOT KEY BOOKS
80–81 Wimpole St, London W1G 9RE
www.hotkeybooks.com

A CIP catalogue record for this book is available from the British Library.

ISBN: 978-1-4714-0786-4
also available as an ebook

1

This book is typeset using Atomik ePublisher
Printed and bound in Great Britain by Clays Ltd, Elcograf S.p.A.

Hot Key Books is an imprint of Bonnier Books UK
www.bonnierbooks.co.uk

1

Blue Command

Rio de Janeiro, Brazil. 1700 hours.

'What the hell are these *kids* doing here?'

Silence.

'Do you think I'm an idiot?'

Silence.

'I thought you were bringing me the SAS. Is this some kind of joke?'

Max Johnson knew that Sir Alistair Sinclair, the British ambassador to Brazil, was an experienced diplomat. Before his posting to South America, he had represented Her Majesty's Government in India, Switzerland and Gabon. Max had watched a YouTube video of Sir Alistair giving a speech to the United Nations. He came across as charming, well-spoken and tactful.

But right now his diplomatic skills were not on display. His brow was furrowed, his eyes flinty. He looked at the five teenagers standing in front of him with undisguised contempt. 'My son is missing, and you're wasting my time with a bunch of *children*?'

He had a point, Max thought. If Sir Alistair had been expecting the SAS, in full black gear with masks and weapons and body armour, it would be an unpleasant surprise to be presented with five scruffy teenagers in jeans, T-shirts and trainers.

But the ambassador had clearly never heard of the Special Forces Cadets. Which meant he had no idea just how capable they were.

Max glanced along the line. Next to him was Sami, a slight Syrian boy with short black hair, brown eyes and dark skin. He wore his usual earnest expression, as though he was genuinely trying to understand the ambassador's point of view.

Beside Sami was Abby: pale skin, blue eyes, thick, shiny, dishevelled brown hair and double cartilage piercing in her left ear. Abby was never more than a breath away from a sarcastic comment in her pronounced Northern Irish accent. She looked like she was trying very hard to stop herself remarking upon the ambassador's behaviour. Max could see her lips twitching.

Lili was next to her. Chinese, with long, straight, dark hair and a cold expression, Lili was the most intelligent person Max had ever met. She had a photographic memory and a remarkable facility for learning languages. In the past two months she had picked up Spanish and Portuguese to go alongside her Russian, English, Arabic and native Mandarin.

She stared at the ambassador, one eyebrow raised.

Which was more than could be said for Lukas, who stood to her right. Lukas was a black kid from the rough end of Los Angeles. When he thought someone was being foolish, he would say so. His lip was curled. 'Yeah,' he said. 'A bunch of children. Maybe we should leave you to it. You're an adult, after all. You could be in and out, no questions –'

'Hush, Lukas,' said one of the other adults in the room. Her name was Angel. She had fiery red hair tied in a tight ponytail. She stood with Woody, who had sandy hair, a ruddy face and laughter lines bracketing his mouth.

If the third adult had any laughter lines – and that was distinctly unlikely – nobody had seen them for years. Hector had a full greying black beard, dark eyes and a stormy face. He, Woody and Angel were known as the Watchers to the cadets. But at the moment they weren't watching their charges. They were watching the ambassador, who seemed outraged by Lukas's comment.

'How dare you talk to me like that, young man?' the ambassador said. 'Don't you know who I am?'

Abby held up one finger. 'Hang on,' she said. 'I think I know this one.'

There was a pause as everyone turned to look at her.

'Room service?'

'Abby!' Hector barked. Abby looked down. Hector stepped towards the ambassador. 'Sit down,' he said.

They were in a suite on the thirty-fifth floor of the Hilton Hotel in Rio de Janeiro, but they could have been anywhere. The curtains were closed. The door was locked from the

3

inside. The air conditioning meant it was neither hot nor cold. There were two sofas, a desk and a chair, and doors leading to the bedroom and bathroom. The ambassador sat on one of the sofas and immediately appeared to regret doing so. Hector towered over him. The ambassador stood up again, brushing the lapels of his suit jacket. He opened his mouth as if about to deliver another criticism, but closed it again after a glance at Hector. He seemed to sense that the balance of power had changed. Max almost felt sorry for the man. He too had been on the receiving end of Hector's ferocity and he knew it wasn't a comfortable place to be.

Of course, the ambassador had his own reasons for being panicked and upset. That was why the cadets had been airlifted from their base, Valley House in the wilds of Scotland, and transported by plane to Rio.

'My son is *missing*,' the ambassador said to Hector, his voice plaintive. 'You have to find him.'

'We've been briefed,' Hector said. 'But I want to hear it direct from you. Please, sit down.'

To encourage him, Hector sat on the sofa. The ambassador joined him. He took a moment to gather his thoughts before speaking again. 'My son's name is Tommy. He's fifteen.' He frowned. 'Since his mother died he's been . . . there's really no other way to put it. He's been a problem child.'

'What do you mean? What kind of problems?'

'I just can't get through to him,' the ambassador said. 'He won't talk to me, he's not interested in his school work . . .'

'Sounds like me on a good day,' Abby muttered.

The ambassador didn't seem to hear her. 'The embassy is in Brasilia, the capital,' he said. 'But I had to come to Rio a week ago to meet a UK trade delegation. Tommy didn't want to join me. He sulked all the way here, headphones on, staring at his phone . . .'

'Sounds pretty normal –' Abby started to say.

'Will you give it a rest, Abby?' Angel chided. 'The man's son is missing.' Her words seemed to have more effect than Hector's. Abby looked embarrassed.

'We checked into the hotel and he didn't leave his room for two days. Then, four nights ago . . .' The ambassador clicked his fingers. 'He vanished. Nobody saw what happened to him. My security people have examined the hotel's CCTV footage and there's no sign of him leaving.'

'Easily done,' Angel said, 'if you spend a little time checking where the cameras are.'

The ambassador frowned at Angel's interruption. 'He's been missing ever since.' He closed his eyes and pinched the bridge of his nose. 'Twenty-four hours ago, the Rio authorities told my embassy that he is being held in the Complexo do Alemão favela – and his captors know who he is. We expect a ransom demand, which the UK authorities will refuse to pay on principle.'

Hector turned to the cadets. 'We don't expect the ransom demand to come in for a few days. They'll want to have time to make it look like Tommy is in a bad state before they send it. We got the call twenty hours ago, as soon as it became clear that Tommy was in the favela. You know what the favelas are, right?'

'Slums?' Max said. He felt alert. They had used the flight to Rio to sleep and avoid jetlag, so this was the first briefing they'd been given. It was important to take in every last detail.

Hector nodded. 'They're built on the hillsides on the outskirts of Rio. Huge, sprawling areas, very poor. The houses are constructed on top of each other – literally, sometimes. The well-to-do parts of Rio you've seen so far? The beach and the palm trees and the skyscrapers?' He shook his head. 'Nothing like the favelas. Some of them are less dangerous than others, but some are real no-go areas.'

'Let me guess,' Abby said. 'The favela where we think Tommy is, that's a nice quiet one, right?'

'It's the worst,' Hector said. 'Even the regular Rio police don't venture into Alemão.'

'Why not?' Sami asked, looking perplexed.

'Because it's more than their lives are worth. The favela is riddled with gangs. The dominant gang call themselves Blue Command.' As he spoke, Hector glanced at Lukas, who looked at the floor. Lukas came from a gang background, which he felt embarrassed – even ashamed – of. Hector moved on. 'Blue Command import drugs from the Mexican cartels. They distribute these drugs around the favela. But that's not the only way they make their money. They run what we'd call in the UK protection rackets. That's when they take money from locals in return for providing protection from other gangs. But if the locals don't pay up, they get attacked by Blue Command.'

'Nice,' Lili said.

'You haven't heard the worst of it,' Angel said. 'Blue Command also run a people-trafficking business. They abduct *favelados* – people who live in the favelas – and sell them on to rich families in rural parts of South America.'

'Like slaves?' Sami asked, his expression hard.

'Like slaves,' Angel said.

There was a long silence. The ambassador broke it. 'Damn it, I thought you were sending in the SAS! I *asked* for the bloody SAS.'

Hector continued talking as if he hadn't spoken. 'It's a tough life, being a gang member in Blue Command. Kids are recruited early. At the age of eight – younger, sometimes. And their life expectancy is short. Gun crime, drugs . . . Once you're in the gang, your chances of making it past the age of twenty are slim. Blue Command is run by adult gang members, but the foot soldiers, lookouts, mules and gunmen – they're all teenagers and younger.' He turned to the ambassador. 'We can't send adults in to penetrate Blue Command's stronghold,' he said. 'The gang's commanders have several defensive cordons around them. Unfamiliar adults will stick out a mile. But this lot?' He pointed at the cadets. 'Nobody will pay them any attention. We don't know where Blue Command are keeping your son. This team will have a better opportunity to get closer to him in a day than adult forces would manage in a week.'

The ambassador blinked at him. 'You're *insane*,' he said. 'Your team? They should be revising for their GCSEs, not . . .' He shook his head in disbelief. 'I can't believe this is happening. Will somebody get me Number Ten on the phone?'

There was another long silence. 'All right then, everyone,' Abby said at last. 'You heard the fella. Let's go.'

'Wait . . . what?' the ambassador stuttered.

'We'll be off,' said Max. He understood what Abby was doing. 'Like you said, we have GCSEs to revise for, and Abby's physics really stinks.'

'He's not wrong,' Abby said. 'I guess I've been spending too much time practising HALO jumps from 25,000 feet.'

'And weapons training,' Sami added with a half-smile. 'You'll never pass physics if you waste your time spending three hours a day on the firing range.'

'True,' Abby said with a rueful nod. 'And I wouldn't want to be going up against these Blue Command kids without a solid understanding of Boyle's law. So come on, we'd better get moving.' The cadets headed towards the door. 'What the hell is Boyle's law, by the way?' Abby muttered.

'Wait,' the ambassador snapped. He looked at Hector. 'HALO jumps?' he said in a hushed voice. 'Weapons training? Who *are* these kids?'

'They're the people who are going to get your son out of the favela,' Hector said quietly. 'If you'll stop treating them like idiots and let them do their jobs, that is.'

'You've been sent by British Intelligence?' the ambassador said.

Hector nodded.

'Then I guess I don't have a choice.'

'You don't,' Hector said. He stared at the ambassador. 'I need to ask you a question,' he said, 'and I need you to give me an honest answer. Do you think your son went to the favela of his own accord?'

The ambassador didn't answer immediately. He bowed his head, then nodded.

'Why?'

'It's well known to be . . .'

'Go on.'

'To be a place where it's easy to buy drugs. He must have known how dangerous the Alemão favela is. Drugs are the only reason I can think he would risk going there.' He sniffed. 'Tommy is a high-maintenance child.'

Silence.

Hector stood up. 'I need to ask you to leave now,' he told the ambassador. 'I have to brief the team more fully. We'll have your lad back within forty-eight hours. You have my word.' It didn't sound like Hector, and Max suspected he was just saying that to give the ambassador hope.

The ambassador stood up. Pale-faced, he looked at the Watchers and each of the cadets in turn. Then he shook his head, as though he couldn't quite believe the situation he found himself in, and headed silently for the door. He unlocked the door and left without a word.

The door clicked shut. Woody locked it again.

'So,' Abby said brightly, 'bust into the most dangerous favela in Rio, dodge the gangs and rescue the ambassador's son. Easy peasy lemon squeezy.'

Hector gave her a hard look. 'Shut up and listen,' he said. 'You need to understand what you're *really* up against.'

9

2

Death Squad

'It's the police, isn't it?'

Lili had said little. But as usual, when she did speak, everyone listened. Hector gave her a sharp look.

'You said even the *regular* Rio police don't venture into this favela,' Lili continued. 'What about the *non*-regular Rio police?'

'Very good, Lili,' Hector muttered. He glanced towards the door, as if checking that the ambassador had definitely left. 'Have any of you ever heard of the BOPE?' He pronounced it 'bopay'.

There was no response from the cadets.

'It's the tactical unit of Rio's military police. They call themselves a police unit, but they're far more than that. The BOPE is largely made up of former paratroopers and ex-Special Forces soldiers. They have their own gruelling selection process and they're kitted out like SF soldiers, not police officers. We're talking assault rifles, fragmentation grenades, the works. They have their own armoured fighting vehicles. One of them's called the *Caveirão*, or "Big Skull". Another's called the *Pacifador*.'

'The Peacemaker,' Lili translated. 'Doesn't sound like a very accurate name.'

'It's not,' said Hector. 'The role of the BOPE is to target drug gangs in the favelas. They have a shoot-to-kill policy for all members of drug gangs and their associates. Same goes for anyone posing a threat to civilians. The BOPE are brought in for riot control and to serve high-risk arrest warrants. They provide high-power fire support in firearms situations. They're also highly trained in hostage rescue, so they can extract police officers or other people who have been abducted by the drug gangs.'

'So why aren't the BOPE rescuing the ambassador's son,' Lukas said, 'if they're so hard?'

'I'm getting to that.' Hector took a moment to gather his thoughts. 'Often, people attracted to serving in units like the BOPE are not always on the side of the angels. The BOPE guys – and they are all guys – operate a "shoot first, ask questions later" policy. We know they carry spare firearms to plant on civilian corpses who get caught in the crossfire.'

'Why would they do that?' Sami asked.

'Obvious, isn't it?' said Abby.

'Not to me,' Sami said.

'So they can say that the person they shot was about to fire at them, even if they were completely innocent. Right, Hector?'

11

'Right,' Hector said. 'There have been a number of incidents of falsified crime scenes like this, often involving innocent teenagers who have found themselves in the wrong part of the favela at the wrong time. Make no mistake: the BOPE are aggressive, excessively violent and relaxed about the idea of collateral damage. People in Rio refer to them not as a police unit but as a death squad.'

'Sounds to me,' Max said, 'like that's more of a problem for Blue Command than it is for us.'

'I wish that was true,' Hector said. 'When I said that certain members of the BOPE aren't on the side of the angels, I meant it. Some take out the drug dealers then steal their money, or steal their drugs and sell them on as a side business.'

'That's wrong,' Sami said. He looked genuinely shocked.

'It doesn't stop there. Some of the BOPE are known to sell arms to the gangs. A gang member with an old handgun is one thing. A gang member with an M16 assault rifle is a different proposition. That's what they're packing, and a substantial proportion of their heavy weaponry comes straight from the tactical police unit.'

'What a mess,' Lili said.

'You bet it's a mess,' Hector agreed. 'And it's an even bigger mess where Blue Command are involved.' He walked to the other side of the hotel room and retrieved an iPad from the desk. He swiped it and held it up. The screen showed a Brazilian man, perhaps in his early twenties. He had dark skin and a wild Afro haircut. He wore a tropical shirt and a chunky gold necklace. His smile was crooked, his eyes very blue.

12

'He looks cool,' Abby said. 'Who is he?'

'Right now, I'd say he's the most wanted man in Rio de Janeiro. His name is Antonio Guzman, and he's the leader of Blue Command.' Hector looked directly at Abby. 'And he's really not the kind of guy you'd want to know.'

'Ah, don't worry. I only have eyes for Max.' She sounded sarcastic, but when she slid Max a glance he felt himself blush.

'Guzman is wanted on twelve counts of murder,' Hector continued, 'but he's committed far more than that. He runs Blue Command with an iron fist, and under his leadership the gang is responsible for more crime and suffering in the favela than almost any other organisation in Brazil. Drug dealing, protection rackets, people trafficking . . .' Hector frowned. 'He's evil, and unhinged, but clever,' he said. 'Ordinarily, gangs don't last long in the favela. Whichever gang is in the ascendency gets hit hard and fast by the BOPE. Sure, there's always another gang waiting to take over, but they never have time to get a real foothold before the BOPE come for them. Guzman's thought of a way around that. He's put the BOPE on his payroll.'

The cadets were silent.

'What this means,' Hector continued, 'is that Blue Command effectively have their own Special Forces unit. If any of the less dominant gangs in the favela start flexing their muscles, the BOPE move in and do what they do best.'

'Kill them,' Sami said bleakly.

'Yeah. Kill them.'

13

'And if, say, five foreign teenagers entered the favela with the aim of rescuing one of Blue Command's hostages,' Abby said quietly, 'the BOPE, let me guess, would give them a biscuit and a mug of warm milk and send them on their way. Or, hang on, would they kill them too?'

Hector didn't answer that. Instead, he swiped the iPad again. An image appeared of three corpses on a pavement. Their faces weren't visible, but their clothes were blood-stained. 'These were taken last week,' Hector said. 'The three victims are all under the age of fifteen.'

He let that sink in for a moment before swiping again. A logo appeared. It was circular, with a red circumference and a black interior. On top was a white skull with a dagger driven through the top and emerging from the chin. Two yellow pistols formed a cross behind the skull. '*Faca ne caveira*,' Hector said.

'Knife in the skull,' Lili immediately translated from Portuguese. 'Charming.' She pulled her Special Forces Cadets challenge coin, with its winged star logo, from her pocket, and flicked it like a coin. 'Makes these look kind of tame.'

Another swipe of the iPad. A soldier appeared, dressed in black. He wore body armour and a full military ops waistcoat and belt kit. He had a knee protector on his right leg to protect the joint when he knelt to fire. He was carrying what Max immediately recognised as an M16 assault rifle with laser sights. He wore a black military helmet and a balaclava.

'This is what the BOPE guys protecting Blue Command will look like,' Hector said. 'Note the balaclava.'

'That's not going to stop a bullet,' Lukas said.

'It's not supposed to,' Hector replied. 'Many members of the BOPE actually live in the favelas. For obvious reasons, they're not always popular with the other people who live there. These areas are grindingly poor. Many of the inhabitants of the favela travel into central Rio to work in low-paid, menial jobs. Back home, they have poor sanitation and unreliable electricity. Healthcare is often non-existent. Families live on top of each other, many to a room. Some of the buildings are literally made of cardboard. Everybody knows that the drug gangs make the situation worse. So, when they're on operations, the BOPE guys tend to hide their faces with balaclavas so they can remain anonymous. If they didn't, and ordinary, law-abiding people realised their neighbours were in the pockets of the gangs . . .'

'They wouldn't be law-abiding for much longer,' Lukas said.

'Right,' Hector said. He swiped again. They saw a photograph of a second BOPE officer, taken from a distance. The officer also wore a black balaclava, but this time it bore a silver insignia on the forehead. Hector zoomed in. 'It's a jackal,' he said. 'That's what this guy is known as. The Jackal. We don't know his real name, but he's the guy Guzman pays to keep the rest of the BOPE onside. You want to stay clear of him. Word is, he's the most trigger-happy of the lot.'

'I'm not going to lie, Hector,' Max said. 'Us five against the worst the BOPE and Blue Command can throw at us? It doesn't feel like a fair fight. Will we be armed?'

15

Hector shook his head. 'If I had my way, you would be, but our superiors won't allow it. In any case, it would probably be the wrong call, ops-wise. Your job is to be invisible. Street kids who nobody would look at twice. You can't be that if you're packing assault rifles. You're going in under the radar. That means no firearms.'

'Not even a teensy little handgun?' Abby said.

'No.'

'What if we promise not to shoot anyone?'

'No.'

'What if we *pinky* promise not to shoot anyone?'

'Ask me again, Abby, you'll be on the first flight back to the UK.'

'And miss this lovely opportunity to be killed by Guzman, the Jackal, Blue Command and the Brazilian armed police?' She ticked them off on her fingers. 'Why on earth would I want to do that?'

'You'll have backup,' Angel said. 'Woody and I will set up an ops room on the outskirts of the favela. We'll be able to track your individual locations at all times. If you raise the alarm, we'll move in.'

'If we raise the alarm,' Lili said, 'it might be too late. Those BOPE guys sound like they know what they're doing.'

'And so do you,' Hector said. It wasn't often that their handler paid them a compliment, and Max thought it had an immediate effect on them all. They stood taller and seemed less scared.

'How will we find this Tommy guy, anyway?' Lukas said.

'We don't know exactly where he is,' said Hector. 'But

we do know that Blue Command's operations are focused around the north-east of the favela. You'll find that as you approach it, security gets tough. But it'll be up to you to locate the hostage. You just need to be careful about what questions you ask – and who you ask.'

Hector looked at his watch, then strode over to the window and pulled back the blackout curtain. It was dark outside. 'Come with me,' he said. 'I want to show you something.'

Hector led the cadets and the Watchers from the room. They walked silently along an empty corridor towards the lift. Hector pressed the button that took them to the rooftop bar. After all the talk of favelas and drug gangs, it felt unreal walking into such a glamorous place. There was a long, mirrored cocktail bar at one end of the room, and a pianist played quiet jazz on a shiny black grand piano. Thirty or forty guests were milling around the bar area and by the floor-to-ceiling windows that overlooked the city. Woody ordered lemonades and Hector led the cadets, drinks in hand, to the windows.

The view over the Rio skyline was breathtaking. The lights of the city glowed excitingly across the urban sprawl. There was a spectacular view out to sea – the bay was full of yachts. A bright moon illuminated the water and outlined the surrounding hills. It was beautiful, but Max couldn't work out why Hector had brought them here. A relaxed drink in a swanky hotel bar was hardly his style.

'Can you see what I can see?' Hector said.

Max peered through the glass. He didn't know what their

handler was talking about. Then he heard Lukas whisper something.

'What is it?' Max said. 'What are you –'

And then he saw.

There was a hill in the distance. Its lower slopes were covered with houses, and the glow that emanated from it was less bright than that which bathed the centre of the city. Lights flashed above some of the buildings. 'Are they fireworks?' Max said.

'No,' Lili answered. 'Not fireworks. Gunfire. From the rooftops.'

Sami gave a low whistle. Abby stared. Max said, 'It's like a war zone.'

'It's not *like* a war zone,' Hector said. 'It *is* a war zone. That's tracers you can see. Tourists come and watch the most dangerous favelas from viewing points like this.' He looked around. 'Cocktails and firefights,' he said, in a tone of voice that left nobody in any doubt about what he thought of such people. 'Don't they realise people are dying? It's pathetic.'

Pathetic or not, Max couldn't take his eyes from the faraway firefight. To put yourself in such an environment was borderline crazy. But that was what they were going to do.

'Finish your drinks,' Hector said. 'We mobilise first thing in the morning. You need your sleep.'

He turned and left the bar with Woody and Angel. The cadets glanced nervously at each other, then followed.

3

Guzman and the Jackal

Antonio Guzman was in a good mood. And when Guzman was in a good mood, his lieutenants were in a good mood – because he was less likely to shoot one of them.

He had been in a good mood ever since the English boy, Tommy, had been abducted four nights ago. When they had brought the kid to him, struggling and shouting, Guzman had planned to let his people use him as live target practice. It was always good for the younger ones to get their first kill in early. It got it out of the way and meant they wouldn't hesitate if they had to do it again in future. Guzman had been nine when he murdered his first man. Tommy had only been in Guzman's hands for a couple of hours when another feisty nine-year-old had put a barrel to the hostage's head, ready to take the shot.

But then the Jackal had entered.

The Jackal was Guzman's tame BOPE agent, although perhaps 'tame' was not the right word. He could be as vicious

19

as his boss if he wanted to be, and was almost – *almost* – as feared in the favela as Guzman himself. He always wore a black balaclava with a silver jackal insignia on the forehead. Very few people had ever seen his face.

The Jackal's eyes had been dead and emotionless as Guzman had screamed at him to leave the room. They had barely flickered as Guzman stormed up to him, waving the Uzi submachine gun he always carried.

'It's up to you, Guzman,' the Jackal had said in a lazy voice, 'but I wouldn't shoot that one if I were you.'

Guzman had seen a red mist. 'You think you can tell me who to kill and who not to kill?' he shouted. His voice went higher whenever he got angry. It rose at least an octave now. '*I* pay *you*! Never forget that!'

The Jackal had shrugged. 'Fine,' he said. 'Shoot him, and throw five million reais down the drain.'

Guzman had lowered his Uzi. 'What?'

So the Jackal had explained. An alert had been sent out to all police officers. The son of the British ambassador to Brazil was missing. One of the Jackal's officers had been in the favela when Guzman's gang members had abducted the kid, who had by all accounts simply walked across Rio and straight into the favela. The officer recognised the police picture. Dyed blond hair. Blue eyes. Lanky frame. There was no doubt about it: by chance, Guzman had the ambassador's son, and he was worth a fortune in ransom money.

Now, four days later, Guzman was standing on the rooftop of the building in the heart of the favela that he used as his Blue Command headquarters. It was an ugly concrete structure, guarded on the ground floor by armed men. The immediate vicinity was deserted and quiet: people who lived in the favela knew it was in their best interests to avoid this place. There was an old basketball court below, unused as always. From the roof, Guzman could see over a large portion of the slum. He could see the tumbledown houses, some of them made of brick, some of recycled planks of wood, crates or even cardboard. He could hear traffic and music and somewhere, in the distance, gunfire. He felt like a king looking over his domain, even more so as he fingered his chunky gold necklace.

And a king, he decided, should be able to do what he wanted.

The Jackal had advised him to wait a couple of days before issuing the ransom request. Make them sweat. But that didn't mean Guzman couldn't have some fun with the boy. He called to one of the three guards standing nearby, each of them wearing a Blue Command bandana. 'Bring me the English kid,' he said.

Two minutes later, the hostage was on his knees, his head bowed, the moon casting a shadow across the roof. Guzman stood in front of him. He knew they did not share a language so he grabbed a clump of the kid's bleached blond hair and pulled him to his feet. He was almost as tall as Guzman, but so slight that he made Guzman laugh when he jutted out his chin defiantly.

'You a big man, hey?' he shouted at him in Portuguese. 'You a brave man?'

Guzman aimed his Uzi at the ground, just to the right

of the boy's feet. He fired a burst of 9mm rounds. The boy jumped back in fear. Guzman barked with laughter, then fired again. 'Dance, brave boy!' he shouted. He had seen someone say that in a movie, and it amused him to repeat it. He looked over at his guards. 'Look at him dance!' he shouted. He gave a high-pitched giggle.

The guards laughed as well, one of them more than the other two. When Guzman fired his Uzi for a third time, the blond boy almost collapsed backwards into this guard. The guard licked his lips, then spun the boy around and kneed him hard in the groin. The boy doubled over and the guard raised his knee into his face. The boy collapsed in a heap on the ground, groaning with pain, his face bleeding.

The guard laughed even harder, then grinned at Guzman. But his smile disappeared when he saw the look on Guzman's face.

Guzman sneered. Nobody was laughing now. He walked up to the guard in silence. The guard glanced at his two mates, but they had both taken a step backwards, as if they wanted nothing to do with him.

Guzman stood close to the guard. 'What do you think you're doing?' he whispered.

The guard swallowed hard. 'I-I'm sorry. I thought –'

'Your job isn't to think,' Guzman said. 'Your job is to do as you're told. Who told you to hit him? Who said you could play my game?'

'Nobody. I-I'm sorry, boss. I –' He looked down to see Guzman's Uzi pointing at his belly. 'Please . . .' he said.

It was the last word he spoke.

Guzman fired. The bullets threw the guard backwards. He landed on his back, dead, blood flowing from his stomach.

Guzman glanced at the other two guards. 'Get rid of him,' he said. He pointed at the English boy, who was hyperventilating with terror. 'And lock this stupid kid up. The sooner we get some ransom money for him, the sooner we can kill him.'

He turned his back on the carnage and returned to the edge of the rooftop, where he looked over the favela once more. He was in a bad mood now, and he wanted to be left alone.

4

Bullet Hole

Back at Valley House, where Max and the other cadets lived, trained, ate and slept, their quarters were functional. Hard beds, spartan living areas. They were nothing like the comfortable hotel room Max found himself in that night. The bed was large and soft, the bathroom bright and marble-clad, the lighting soft, the minibar filled with chocolate and crisps. Max didn't like it. Valley House was home to him now. There was something deeply reassuring about its lack of creature comforts. The cadets spent their time in that bleak Scottish valley learning skills that would keep them alive in the toughest circumstances. Their surroundings were an extension of that: utilitarian. A reminder of who they were and what they could expect from this part of their lives. This hotel room, cocooning him with its soft furnishings and warm blankets, was a lie. On the streets of the favela, surrounded by ruthless criminals and armed personnel, he needed to be encased in granite. He spent a long, sleepless night.

Before dawn, there was a knock on his door. Max fumbled for the lamp, his head stuffy and his eyes bleary, then crawled out from under his covers wearing just his boxer shorts. He opened up to find Woody, smiling as always. 'Looking good, Max. Can I come in?'

Max stepped aside so the Watcher could enter.

'You get any sleep?'

'I think I got half an hour just before three.'

'Quite a good night then,' Woody said without a hint of irony. 'These hotel rooms kind of suck, huh?'

'Once, I'd have loved them.'

'Yeah, well, we'll be back home soon. You need to get dressed.'

Max's clothes were slung over the back of the armchair by his bed. He walked towards the chair.

'Not those,' Woody said. 'You need to look like a favela kid.' He indicated the bag he'd brought into the room. 'Put these on. Meet us downstairs in ten minutes.'

Woody left the room, leaving Max to unpack the bag. There was an old pair of baggy jeans and a yellow Brazil football top. Old sandals and a baseball cap. The clothes were grubby and reeked of sweat. Max wondered where the Watchers had sourced them, then decided not to think too hard about that. The football top felt greasy as he pulled it on. He wore the baseball cap backwards and checked himself in the mirror. Did he look like a favela street kid? The clothes looked right, but his skin was white. He knew that there were many different skin colours in the favelas, but he was pleased to find a final item in the bag: a blue wrap, halfway between a bandana and an Arabic *keffiyeh*. Max wrapped it around his head so that only his eyes were exposed. In the dim light of the hotel room, he suddenly looked like a different person. He hoped the transformation would be as convincing on the streets.

He unwrapped the scarf and let it hang around his neck. Leaving the rest of his stuff where it was, he headed into the corridor. Sami was emerging from the next room. The dark smudges under his eyes told Max that his friend had slept just as poorly. Maybe that wasn't a bad thing. Max guessed that the average favela street kid was unlikely to look fresh and well rested. Sami was dressed like Max: in a plain green T-shirt instead of the Brazil football top, but in similar jeans and sandals and a darker blue wrap. 'This is not my style,' he said with characteristic seriousness.

'You're nailing it, mate,' Max said. 'Come on, let's get downstairs.'

The others, with the exception of Hector, were waiting in the hotel foyer. They were all dressed in nondescript clothes which, although they weren't a million miles from the clothes they would normally wear, somehow made them look substantially different. Each of them carried a blue head-wrap similar to Max and Sami's. Other than the concierge, they were the only people about.

'Where's Hector?' Max asked quietly. Angel nodded at the revolving doors at the front of the hotel. A white van, dented along one wing, was pulling up outside. The cadets followed Woody and Angel out of the hotel and into the back of the van. There was seating along both sides, and no windows. There were five rucksacks waiting for them. The only light came from a dim bulb. The cadets took their places facing each other and the van moved off.

'Take a rucksack each,' Woody said. 'You'll find some basic supplies in there. Medical packs, water, paracord, cable ties, a knife, and an extra surprise I'll show you when we reach our destination. Hector's going to drop us on the edge of the Alemão favela. We expect to be there at 0530 hours. There will be people around, but they'll mostly be workers making their way into central Rio. The gang members and street kids tend to be busy at night, so they sleep late. Activity starts again around mid-afternoon. Our drop-off point is a safe house. It's owned by a Brazilian family who are paid by the British Embassy to deliver information about gang and police movements to British Intelligence.'

'How do we know we can trust them?' Lukas said. The cadets had, in the past, learned the hard way that in their line of work, trusting the wrong person could have serious consequences.

'You really want to know?'

'Of course.'

'They've taken money for information on Blue Command and the BOPE. Having done that once, they know they're vulnerable. British Intelligence can find ways of informing the gang what the family have done. If that happened, they'd have hours to get out of the favela, if that.'

'We're blackmailing them?' Sami asked, clearly aghast.

'If that's the word you want to use,' Angel said.

'What word would *you* use?' Lili said.

'It's just the way the world is, okay?' Angel said. 'Get used to it. In any case, my understanding is that the family are on board. Nobody needs to blackmail anybody.'

There was an uncomfortable silence before Woody started talking again. 'We'll set up an ops centre in the safe house. Angel and I will be there at all times. We'll be monitoring your position via the GPS chips in your phones. Each phone has an encrypted calling app. If there's an emergency, launch the app, dial 111 and we'll mount a rescue mission. But that must be a last resort. Your mission is to locate the ambassador's son and extract him to a school – Escola Rodrigues Leandro in the north-west corner of the favela. We'll brief you on its exact location when we reach the safe house. Once you're on the school roof, you'll contact Hector by dialling 222. He'll scramble a helicopter to pick you all up from the roof.'

'Wouldn't it be better,' Lili said, 'to have the helicopter pick us up closer to Tommy's location?'

Woody shook his head. 'Blue Command are heavily armed. There was an incident a while back when they shot down a helicopter flying over their turf. We can't risk that happening. The ambassador's son is bound to be deep in Blue Command territory. You have to get him somewhere safer.'

'You all have head-wraps,' Angel said. 'It's kind of a fashion thing in the favela. If you want to disguise yourself as regular citizens, use those. But you might also want these.' She handed out blue bandanas. 'Only Blue Command personnel wear these,' she said. 'Either covering their hair or the lower half of their face. Put them on now.'

28

Silently, the cadets wrapped the bandanas around their faces. Max's breath felt hot under the material. He examined the others. Having their faces obscured made them look threatening, but they all had a hint of wariness in their eyes as they glanced at each other. Max had come to know them well, and he could sense that they were as anxious as him.

The van slowed down. Max felt his anxiety bite. The vehicle came to a halt. Woody and Angel opened the back of the van and daylight streamed in, stabbing Max's eyes. Dawn had broken. 'Come on,' Angel said. 'Quickly.'

The cadets followed the Watchers out of the van. They found themselves in a deserted street on a steep hill. There were concrete buildings on either side. Some were painted in shades of white and orange that had grown dirty with age. Others were bare concrete. Most of the buildings were plastered with spray-painted graffiti: Portuguese slogans that Max was unable to translate but which Lili seemed to be reading intently. One particular slogan seemed to demand her attention.

'What does it say?' Max asked.

'It says, "The police will die",' Lili said.

The van had stopped outside a bar called the Cafe Tricolor. It didn't look very welcoming. Like many of the other buildings along the road, the cafe's frontage was obscured by heavily padlocked metal shutters, which were also covered in spray paint. Overhead there was a tangled network of cables. Max assumed they were power lines, as they led to each of the houses in turn. But they did not look as if they had been installed professionally. Some of the lines sagged badly, others had exposed wire at ramshackle junction boxes and some seemed to be entering buildings through open windows.

Max could hear a male voice shouting somewhere, but he couldn't see its owner. There were no people in the street at this early hour, but there were a couple of parked cars in view. An old white VW campervan was parked against one of the bare concrete buildings, its front right tyre flat. Beyond it was a red saloon car, beaten up, with an empty roof rack.

On the other side of the road, opposite the Cafe Tricolor, was an alleyway. Woody and Angel headed straight for it and the cadets followed. As Max reached the entrance to the alleyway, he noticed something on the front wall of the adjacent orange building. It was a hole, big enough to fit his fist into. Sami, who was behind him, said, 'It's a bullet hole. They were everywhere in Syria when I was growing up. There were many people with guns, but they weren't skilled. Stray bullets hit buildings all the time. It will be the same here, I think. We'll have to be careful.'

Max nodded his agreement, then followed the others down the alleyway. It led to the back of the orange building. Here there was a rough courtyard with high breezeblock walls and an external metal staircase spiralling up to the first floor of the building. Two feral cats sat on the staircase. They scampered away as soon as the cadets appeared. Angel climbed the staircase and rapped quietly on the door at the top. It opened almost immediately and she gestured at the others to follow. They clattered up the staircase and filed inside.

They found themselves in a room that covered the entire floor of the building. There was an open staircase against one wall leading to the floor above. Max assumed that the sleeping quarters of the family who lived here must be up there, because this was a communal living area. A couple of patched sofas sat in the middle of the room, and an old electric oven against the right-hand wall. In pride of place was a TV. It was not a flat-screen, but an old-fashioned boxy one on a wooden unit. A power cable and an aerial snaked to it from the open window. The TV was on, but all it showed was snowy interference. A small boy stood in front of it, pointing a remote control at the screen. His head was silhouetted by the glow and he was shaking the remote, as if perplexed by the lack of a picture.

The little boy was not the only person in the room. There were four others: two parents and two teenagers, a boy and a girl, who looked like twins. The parents had friendly faces, but they were lined with worry. The mother ushered the guests into the room – 'Quickly, quickly!' – then shut the door behind them. The two teenagers lurked awkwardly by the open staircase, and the boy didn't take his eyes from the TV screen. He tried to change the channel with no success.

The father was a stocky man wearing knee-length shorts and a grubby string vest. He shook everybody's hands in turn. 'Welcome, welcome,' he said. 'Our house is yours. Unwrap your scarves but please, do not leave and do not make a noise. If the BOPE find out that you are here, or the gangs . . .' He shook his head as if to indicate that this would be a terrible outcome. 'I am Manuel, and this is my wife Marta. These are our twins, Leonardo and Verissimo. And this is Pepe.' He turned to the boy and said something sharply in Portuguese. The boy turned. He had a chubby, adorable face. Looking crestfallen, he replied to his father in Portuguese and then, with obvious reluctance, switched off the TV.

'He's football crazy!' said Manuel. 'If he can't play, he watches. If he can't watch, he plays!' He pointed at Max's Brazil football shirt. 'One day,' he announced, 'he will be the new Pele! My boy, he can put a ball in the corner of the net from the halfway line!'

Max looked over at the boy, unable to help replaying Hector's voice in his head. *It's a tough life, being a gang member in Blue Command. Kids are recruited early. At the age of eight – younger, sometimes. And their life expectancy is short. Gun crime, drugs . . . Once you're in the gang, your chances of making it past the age of twenty are slim.*

He thought of the bullet hole in the front wall of the building. If the bullet that made it could do that to concrete, what would it do to a little boy? Max wondered if Pepe would make it to professional footballing age.

He turned to Angel and Woody. 'What do we do now?' he said.

'We set up,' said Angel. 'And we wait.'

5

Pepe's Plan

Woody and Angel each had a shoulder bag, from which they removed a laptop in a hard, scuffed case and a satellite phone. They set these up on a table near the window, propping the sat phone on the sill so it had line of sight to the sky. They logged into their system, then handed each of the cadets a phone on which individual facial recognition software had been set up.

'Secure and encrypted,' Angel told them. 'Keep them on you. That's how we'll track your position.'

'There's an app on the home page of each phone,' Woody continued, 'next to the encrypted calling app. It's called Fogo Cruzado. It means Crossfire. It's designed to pinpoint the location of any gunfire in the Rio de Janeiro area in real time. The locals use it so they know which areas to avoid.'

'Sounds more exciting than Candy Crush,' Abby said.

'Saves more lives than Candy Crush too. Keep an eye on it.'

The Watchers spread a satellite image of the favela out on the table. Using a red marker, Woody circled their current position in the south, then drew a circle to the north-east with a diameter of about 500 metres. 'This area is Blue Command's turf,' he said. 'You'll see that there are only a handful of streets that head into this area.' He indicated five different entry points. 'You'll need to access their territory using one of these.'

'But you *must* be careful,' Manuel said. He was loitering behind the cadets, holding Pepe's hand. 'Those entrances are often blocked. Armed men. They do not let anyone in without checking them first.'

'We'll need a distraction,' Lukas said.

'Right,' Woody agreed. 'Max, give me your rucksack.' He reached into Max's bag and pulled out what looked like a spray can. 'We can't give you live ammunition, but we can give you these. Do you know what they are?'

'Flashbangs,' Max said immediately.

'Exactly. They're grenades that make an enormous noise and a blinding flash of light. Harmless otherwise. There's one each. Use them carefully to distract your enemy. When you're within the Blue Command cordon, you'll have to work out a way to locate the target. Once you've done that, you need to extract him to this location here.' He drew another circle around a large building in the north-east of the favela. 'You need to study this map carefully. Commit it to memory.'

Max had already started to do that. Back at Valley House, they had played a number of games designed to improve their memory and speed of recall. One of these was Kim's game. The cadets had learned that in an old book by Rudyard Kipling, Kim was a child spy who had been taught to become observant by being shown a tray full of jewels. The tray was covered and Kim had to describe all the jewels very precisely. As time passed, more objects were put on the tray for him to remember, and the better his power of recall became.

'You can forget about jewels,' Hector had said with his characteristic bluntness. 'But Kim's game has been used by soldiers for more than a hundred years now. If it's good enough for them, it's good enough for you.' Together, the cadets had become expert. They had learned to remember the order of a pile of cards, or a sequence of letters. They had learned to recognise faces and to distinguish between many people's voices. And of course they had been given maps to scrutinise and memorise all the smallest details they displayed. It had even become a bit of a competition between them. Lili was the best – she had a photographic memory. But they had all become highly skilled.

As Max studied the map, he was grateful for the interminable rounds of Kim's game Hector had made them play. It had seemed over the top at the time, but now he found the details of the favela's layout imprinting themselves on his brain, as if his mind was taking a photograph. He found himself automatically estimating the distance to the centre of Blue Command's stronghold – about a kilometre. He calculated the most efficient route from that part of the favela to Escola Rodrigues Leandro, their pick-up point. He closed his eyes and tried to re-create the satellite map in his mind. It was almost as clear to him as if he had his eyes wide open.

'Why don't we go now?' Lukas said. 'What's the point in waiting?'

'The gangs and the street kids come out at night,' Angel said. 'It's easier to melt into a crowd when there's more people who look like you. Here, you need to see this.' She brought up a new picture on the laptop. 'This is the most recent image we have of Tommy, so you can recognise him when you see him.'

The cadets examined the picture. Tommy had a thin face. Almost gaunt. He had piercing blue eyes and had dyed his hair blond. 'Kind of cute,' Abby observed. She glanced over at Max as she said it. Was it Max's imagination, or had she blushed? He felt an unfamiliar lurch in his stomach. It was something to do with the way Abby had just looked at him.

He turned his attention back to the image and committed it to memory. Lukas and Sami were doing the same. Abby and Lili had already wandered away from the briefing table. The twins had disappeared upstairs, but Pepe was still in the main room. He had some paper and colouring pens and was sprawled on the floor, drawing. They crouched down and joined him, and before long there was a lot of giggling going on. Manuel walked up to the others. 'The twins and Marta are upstairs,' he said. 'They are shy and don't speak much English.' He looked fondly at Pepe, who was playing with the girls. 'It's nice to see him enjoying himself,' he said. 'He plays football with his friends in the favela every evening, but it's not much of a life.'

'Aren't you worried –' Max started to say.

'Worried about what, young man?'

'Well, it's just that, from what I understand, Blue Command like to recruit members when they're very young. Aren't you worried they might try to recruit Pepe?'

A wan smile crossed Manuel's face. 'It's a worry, of course. But Pepe, I think, is sensible. His mother and I tell him often that when youngsters like him join the gangs, more often than not they end up paying the ultimate penalty.' He looked over at Pepe. 'He's a good kid,' he said, and chuckled. 'He spends too much time watching TV, of course, when it is available.'

'Is your TV broken?' Woody said. 'Maybe I could look at it for you.'

Manuel smiled. 'The TV is fine. But the gangs control them, just like they control the electricity.'

'I don't get you,' Max said.

Manuel pointed at the cables coming into through the window. 'Most of the electricity in the favela is stolen. The gangs illegally connect cables to the grid and supply it to individual houses. For a price, of course. The same goes for the TV. Blue Command hack pay-to-view television channels and distribute them to almost all the televisions in the favela. It's football, mainly. Some movies, some kids' TV. It's Guzman's way of bribing the people, making himself more popular, so we turn a blind eye to his other behaviour.' He scowled. 'As if it was possible to do that, when they are also shooting children in the streets.'

'So why isn't it working now?' Lukas asked. 'The TV, I mean.'

'The authorities have done something. Something . . .' He waved his arms in the air, clearly searching for a word. 'Something *technical*. They do not dare to enter Blue Command's territory, so they must attack them in other ways. This is one of them. They have stopped the broadcast of TV across the favela so Blue Command can't claim the credit for providing it.' He glanced over at Pepe again, who was now being tickled by Abby. 'He's a good kid, but he misses his football,' he said.

The gunfire started around midday.

It sounded like fireworks in the distance. The cadets exchanged a long look, but the Brazilian family didn't seem concerned. 'We can tell from the sound how far away it is,' Manuel explained. 'That is not in our neighbourhood. It is not a danger for us.'

'It's a danger for us,' Lukas muttered. 'That's coming from the north-east, where we're heading in a few hours.'

Max checked the app on his phone. Sure enough, an icon had appeared in that area, indicating gunfire. The sound subsided after a few minutes. The cadets went back to waiting. Abby and Lili were playing Kim's game with Pepe, using a pack of cards.

'Kid's got a good memory,' Abby said. 'Give it five years, he'll find Hector on his doorstep trying to recruit him.' She grinned. 'Don't go with the nasty man, Pepe. Not unless you like running for twenty miles with rocks in your backpack.'

Pepe clearly didn't understand what she was saying, but

he giggled nonetheless. He high-fived Abby, who said, 'Me and Pepe are buddies now.'

The family gave them some food – a meat stew and bread. From time to time there was more gunfire in the distance. Sometimes it was a little closer, sometimes further away. It did nothing for Max's nerves as the hour of their departure grew nearer. At 1600 hours, Woody and Angel fired up their laptop and checked that the cadets' GPS locators were operational. The cadets checked the favela map again, along with pictures of Tommy and Guzman.

At quarter to five, Pepe scurried upstairs and returned with his football. He spoke earnestly to his dad in Portuguese, then hugged Lili and Abby before hurrying to the door by which they'd all entered.

'Where's he going?' Angel said sharply.

'To play football with his friends,' Manuel said. 'One day, he will be the new P—'

'He should stay here,' Angel interrupted.

'He'll be safe. He knows where to go and where not to go.'

'I'm not talking about *him*. He might mention us to his friends.'

Manuel shook his head rapidly. 'He understands to be quiet. It will not be a problem.' Before Angel could say anything else, Manuel said something to Pepe in Portuguese and the little boy disappeared.

Angel's face was stormy and she muttered something under her breath. Max had the impression that she was about to run after Pepe.

'Ah, c'mon,' said Abby. 'It's okay for him to go and play

with his friends. He's been cooped up in here all day.'

'We don't have much choice now,' Angel said. 'Woody and I don't want to be seen on the streets, and you lot need to move in fifteen minutes. Headscarves on. It's time to get ready.'

Pepe knew his friends would be waiting for him on the Avenue Santiago. It was the best place to play football because the street was wider than most, and there were few cars, even at busy times of the day. His friends liked having Pepe there because he was the only one with a real leather football. But sometimes he didn't turn up and that was okay too, because they would carry on without him and use a plastic ball.

Of course, what they all wanted was a new pair of football boots. They would probably never wear them on the hard ground of the favela, but would hang them in their shiny glory round their necks like medals. But football boots were expensive, way out of the reach of Pepe and his friends.

Unless . . .

At the end of his road, Pepe didn't turn left. He turned right.

Pepe was a fast runner, and because he was small he could weave quickly in and out of the crowds of people in the favela. It was hot. Many of the men were bare-chested, their T-shirts slung over their shoulders. Some wore vests like his father's. The women wore shorts and carried bags of shopping. There were children too, a few even younger than Pepe. Some were loitering on street corners, smoking cigarettes. Others sat on the kerbside, arguing good-naturedly, or kicking footballs against the graffitied walls of favela buildings. None of them – adult or child – paid Pepe any attention as he sprinted past, heading north-east.

It only took a couple of minutes for his surroundings to grow subtly different. There was more graffiti on the buildings and Pepe, who had learned to read, knew that it consisted of words he was not supposed to know. Brazilian funk music blared from the windows of certain cafes that he knew not to enter. And as for the children? They weren't playing football, and there was nothing good-natured about any arguments he saw. Far from it. Outside a small mini-mart, two broad-shouldered teenagers – their faces covered with blue scarves – were shoving each other. An old lady watched them from the entrance to the shop, her lined face full of concern. But she clearly knew better than to interfere. Pepe skirted the fighting boys and continued running uphill. He slowed down as he passed a man selling grilled meat from a rickety barbecue – it smelled so good! But he didn't stop. He turned left by an old SUV, its doors open, deafening music playing from its loudspeaker. And there, up ahead, he saw what he was looking for.

There were five of them. They wore baseball caps and blue bandanas. The bandanas were folded in half, corner to corner, and tied behind their heads. The material covered their faces below the eyes. Two of them were bare-chested and they had dark tattoos over their arms and chests. The others wore military vests like Pepe had sometimes seen on TV – when it was working, of course. Of these three,

41

two had guns – long ones, slung across their backs. They looked very frightening, but also glamorous. Pepe heard his mother and father's words in his head: *You must stay away from the gangs, Pepe. If you join a gang, you will end up paying the penalty.* It scared him when they said that. But now, he told himself, he shouldn't be scared. These boys would be pleased to hear what he had to say.

He stopped, caught his breath, and walked towards them.

At first, they didn't seem to notice him. Only when he was close enough to see the tattoos on the back of their hands did one of the bare-chested boys turn towards him. He said something that Pepe didn't catch, and the two gunmen turned quickly and raised their weapons. Pepe dropped his football and held his hands in the air. He had seen other people do that when confronted by gunmen from the gangs and he understood why: in the favela, it was possible for a seven-year-old like Pepe to be carrying a gun. He stopped walking and kept the football still with one foot.

'What do you want?' one of the gang members said from behind his bandana. His voice hadn't yet broken.

'I want to tell you something.'

The gang members looked at each other. Pepe couldn't see their mouths, but he could tell that their eyes were smiling.

'What is it?'

Pepe sniffed. He tried to look casual. 'You have to give me some money first,' he said.

The gang members looked at each other again. 'Is this a joke?' one of them spat.

Pepe shook his head. 'Money first, information second.'

42

The image of a shiny new pair of football boots rose in his mind.

One of the bare-chested boys swaggered towards him. He stopped in front of Pepe, then bent down so their eyes were level. Pepe could smell sweat and marijuana, and he noticed that the boy's pupils were very large. It occurred to him that he was making a big mistake and maybe he should run. If he was holding his football, he might have done. But it was on the ground and he wouldn't have time to grab it and sprint . . .

The boy grabbed Pepe's hair, twisting it tight. Pepe squeaked with pain. His other hand curled around Pepe's throat. 'Give me one good reason,' he said, 'why I shouldn't shoot you now like the gutter rat you are.'

Pepe could feel tears forming. All of a sudden, the promise of a new pair of football boots wasn't so alluring. He truly regretted coming here. 'Please,' he whispered. 'I just want to go and play football with my friends.'

The other gang members were walking up. They surrounded him. The guy who had his throat said, 'What information?'

'It's nothing. It isn't important.'

The guy looked up at one of the others. 'Shoot him,' he said.

Pepe's eyes bulged as one of the guys pointed his weapon at Pepe's head. His whole body went cold. His skin tingled. 'No,' he squeeked. 'I just want to go and play football.' Tears trickled down his cheeks.

'What information?' the bare-chested guy repeated.

'There are some teenagers,' Pepe whispered. 'They are British. They came to our house. I heard them talking about . . .'

'About what?'

'About Guzman.'

'What were they saying?'

'I-I can't remember.'

'Think. Think very hard.' The gun guy pressed the barrel of his weapon against Pepe's forehead.

'They . . . they were saying that they were going to go into Blue Command's area . . .'

'When?'

'Tonight.'

Now the gang members laughed. 'They sound even more stupid than you,' one said.

'Can I go now?' Pepe asked. 'I really want to play football.'

The boy who had him in his grip pulled him even closer. 'What do they look like?'

'There are three boys and two girls. One of the boys is black, one of the girls is Chinese. Please, let me go.'

'Where do you live?'

Pepe stared at him. 'I can't tell you,' he said.

The boy looked up to the gun guy and nodded.

You end up paying the penalty.

'Wait!' Pepe squealed. 'No! I –' He didn't want to say it. He didn't want to tell them where he and his family lived. But he was more scared than he had ever been, and the gunman's finger had moved from the trigger guard to the trigger.

So he told them.

'Opposite the Cafe Tricolor. On the first floor.'

44

The gunman lowered his weapon. He turned to one of the other guys. 'Tell Guzman,' he said. The guy ran off down the street.

The boy let go of Pepe. Pepe staggered backwards. He looked over his shoulder, back the way he'd come. Then he looked at his football. He ran forward and grabbed it, then turned to run away. Then he stopped again. He turned and looked at the gang members. 'You won't hurt my family, will you?'

They didn't answer immediately, then one of them said, 'Sure, we won't hurt your family.'

Pepe couldn't tell if he meant it or not. He decided to believe him. Clutching the ball to his chest, he ran away as fast as he could. He decided that he would go and find his friends. His attempt to earn some money had failed. He would try to forget all about it. The Blue Command boys wouldn't tell his mum and dad or his brother and sister. They had said they wouldn't harm his family, after all.

So it would probably be fine.

6

Simple

1700 hours.

The cadets were preparing to leave.

For the past few minutes, Max had stood at the open window where the power and TV cables entered the house. One by one, the others had joined him to look down at the street below. It was starting to get dark and the cafe opposite, which had been closed during the day, had opened. There were people in the street now, all different ages. Some of them milled around outside the cafe, while others walked purposefully past, clearly on their way home. There was enough of a crowd that the cadets could step outside without attracting attention.

The gunfire they had heard in the distance had stopped, but it was noisy. People were shouting at each other in the street. Some of those shouts were good-natured; others weren't. And there was music. Grinding drumbeats came from the cafe, merging with different beats from elsewhere in the favela. It was chaotic and strangely exciting, but to Max the street throbbed with danger. He felt a tight knot of anxiety in his stomach at the prospect of leaving the safe house.

But it was time. The cadets had their headscarves on and their rucksacks slung across their shoulders. Each of them appeared as a dot on Woody and Angel's laptop. Manuel shook them all by the hand.

'Say goodbye to Pepe for us,' Abby said. 'He's a good kid.'

Manuel bowed his head in acknowledgement. The cadets looked over at Woody and Angel, who stood by the laptop. It struck Max that they looked like anxious parents at the school gate. But when Angel gave the final instruction, she sounded anything but. 'Keep your heads. Stay safe. Trust nobody. Now go.'

They filed out of the room and down the metal staircase to the small courtyard behind the house. 'We should split up into two groups,' Lili said. 'We'll be less noticeable that way.'

'Roger that,' Max agreed. 'You, Lukas and Sami go first. I'll follow with Abby.'

'Does that mean we get a romantic walk through the favela, just you and me?' Abby said. But although her words were light-hearted, she sounded as tense as Max felt.

'Turn right at the end of the street,' Max said, 'then –'

'Then second left,' Lili said. 'We studied the map too, Max.' She looked at Lukas and Sami. 'Let's go.'

Without another word, they moved in single file down the alley and disappeared out into the street.

'How long do we give it?' Abby said.

'A minute,' Max said. 'We don't want to lose sight of them.'

They were silent for a few seconds.

'Hey, Max,' Abby said. 'Did something strike you as strange about the ambassador?'

'What do you mean?'

'I don't know. Like he wasn't telling us everything?'

Max shrugged. 'He was freaked out, I guess. His son's missing. He wasn't expecting a cadet team. But I don't think he'd hold anything back. Not in a situation like this. What parent would do that?'

'Not all parents are as trustworthy as you think they are.'

'Yeah,' Max said. 'Well, I wouldn't know about that.'

Abby put one hand on his shoulder. 'Sorry,' she said. 'I didn't mean –'

'Forget about it,' Max said. 'Come on, we should go.' He moved along the alleyway with Abby following close behind.

The music from the cafe was louder down here in the street. Max knew, as soon as he stepped out of the alleyway, that the headscarves were a blessing and a curse. A woman was approaching. She wore shorts and a T-shirt and held a canvas shopping bag to her chest, and she seemed to be in a rush. As soon as she saw Max and Abby, her expression changed. She frowned and looked away, avoiding their eye. Then she hurried over to the other side of the street in an obvious attempt to have no contact with them.

'She thought we might be gang members,' Abby said quietly.

'Yeah,' Max agreed.

'I thought these scarves were supposed to make us anonymous.'

'Me too. But maybe if they make people stay clear of us, that's good too.'

They could just see the others further up the road. They followed, side by side, keeping themselves to themselves. More than a few people went out of their way to avoid staring at them. Max forced himself to walk with confidence, because to appear timid would be conspicuous if passers-by expected the opposite of them. Abby did the same, walking with shoulders back and head high. They passed several colourfully painted, ramshackle buildings. Some of them were peppered with bullet holes. Max found himself wondering what kind of round would make a hole like that. A 7.62, maybe, fired from a high-powered assault rifle. It only served to heighten the anxiety he felt about the dangers the favela might hold for them.

At the end of the road they turned right into a much busier street. There was a cacophony of voices and the thrum of music was stronger, though Max couldn't tell where it was coming from. There were cars on the road – all of them rather beaten up – and they moved slowly because the crowds of pedestrians didn't seem to distinguish between road and pavement. The network of electricity cables overhead was even busier and more complicated than in the street where the safe house was, and the cables sagged precariously in places. Max heard a faint background hum, and he wondered if it came from the power lines.

There was a rank smell. The stench of sewage. Max remembered that Hector had said the favela suffered from poor sanitation. He noticed plastic waste pipes on the front of some of the houses. They led down to the pavement. Max's skin crawled at the thought of the damp, muddy, sticky patches that spread from the bottom of these pipes. He concentrated on the other cadets, who were still visible ahead through the crowd. Max and Abby moved to the opposite pavement, where it was easier to walk unobstructed. There were a lot of beggars here, mostly male, many of them with missing limbs, scarred faces or even eye patches. They looked to Max like the kind of wounds that were associated with violence, and they were all young. If any of them were older than twenty, he'd have been surprised.

The street was on a steep gradient. They walked uphill, past haphazardly built houses on either side. Some had broken windows; many had roofs constructed from sheets of corrugated iron. There were shops too, and more cafes. Despite the obvious poverty, there was a certain vibrancy. People called and waved to each other over the noise of car horns. The cadets passed a cafe that had salsa music blaring loudly and several stalls outside selling street food: cauldrons of beans and rice, flatbreads with sizzling meat and deep-fried pastries. It smelled enticingly spicy and sweet.

'I could eat some of that,' Abby said, quietly so that her English didn't stand out amid the babble of voices talking Portuguese. But even as she spoke, Max gently grabbed her arm.

'Look,' he said.

A car was parked on their side of the road up ahead. It was a convertible SUV, and it almost seemed to vibrate with the volume of the music blaring from it. Four people were in the car, standing up on the seats so their heads were visible above the vehicle's roof. They had blue bandanas covering the lower part of their faces, and shaved heads. They seemed to repel the flow of pedestrians, who walked around the vehicle, keeping their distance.

'Blue Command?' Abby said.

'I guess so,' Max said. 'Look, the others have crossed the road. We should do the same.'

They crossed the road. An old Brazilian man in a beaten-up car waved a fist at them as they passed in front of his barely moving vehicle. On the other side of the road, they continued to climb, keeping their heads down so that the gang members in the SUV didn't notice them.

They were alongside the SUV when there was a disturbance up ahead. A young boy was sprinting down the hill and knocked an older woman to one side. He was carrying a football. He was running so fast, he almost ran straight into Abby. 'Pepe!' she said, and Max saw that it was the little boy she and Lili had spent most of the day playing with.

Pepe didn't seem at all pleased to see his new friend. Maybe he didn't recognise her voice. He looked up in absolute alarm, took several paces back, then skirted them and continued to run down the hill. Abby watched him go, her head tilted. 'Maybe he's not my new best friend after all,' she said.

'Keep walking,' Max said. The guys in the SUV were looking in their direction. Max could feel their eyes burning into him. He felt like running, but did his best to keep a steady speed and not draw further attention to himself. They moved past the SUV. He was desperate to look back over his shoulder to see if they were still being watched. But a movement like that could scupper the whole operation. He could almost hear Hector's instructions in his head. *Keep your patience. Keep your discipline.* He carried on looking straight ahead and walking slowly. Abby did the same.

But then they heard a shout.

Max's body went cold. He knew beyond question it was the guys in the SUV, and he knew intuitively they were shouting at him and Abby. He heard Abby mutter a swear word under her breath. 'Do we run?' she whispered. 'We've got to be fitter than them, right?'

Max glanced over his shoulder. Two of the guys had jumped down from the SUV and were crossing the road towards them. To run would make them stand out even more, and the gang members would surely chase them . . .

Moments later, the two guys were right in front of them. Max couldn't see the lower part of their faces because of their bandanas, but he could see their eyes flashing. One of them jabbed Max hard in the chest and they gabbled at him in Portuguese. Neither Max nor Abby spoke the language, so they couldn't understand a word.

Defuse the situation, Max told himself. *Step back, be compliant, let them think they're the big guys.* He raised his hands, palms out, as if to say 'I don't want any trouble'. He and Abby took a step backwards. But the guys were still shouting at them. It sounded like they were asking a question. Max and Abby glanced nervously at each other. Maybe, Max thought, the only thing they could do now was run . . .

He looked from side to side. And then he saw Lili.

She was striding up to them. The guys didn't seem to notice her until she was alongside them. She stood in front of Max and Abby. The two guys looked her up and down but fell silent. Lili started talking. To Max, her Portuguese sounded fluent and native. She waved her arms in the air and occasionally pointed at Max and Abby. The two guys, unable to interrupt her, looked at each other and shrugged. Lili didn't let up. Her voice rose and her words came even more quickly. Now it was the turn of the two gang members to raise their hands, but it was almost a gesture of defeat. They retreated back across the road and re-joined their mates in the car.

'Get moving,' Lili told them. 'Don't look back!'

Max and Abby didn't need to be told twice. Sweating heavily, Max followed the two girls up the hill, trying to put as much distance between him and the gang members as possible.

'What did you do there?' Abby asked Lili.

'I talked to them,' Lili said.

'I know that!' Abby retorted. 'What did you say?'

'I told them you were my family,' Lili said. She sounded evasive.

'And that did it?'

'Er, no, not really.'

'So what else did you tell them?' Abby sounded frustrated.

'I, er . . . I told them you were a bit simple.'

Abby stopped. Lili and Max did the same. 'You told them *what*?'

'A bit simple. You know, not quite all there. I figured they wouldn't take you too seriously if they knew that.' She hesitated. 'It just kind of came to me, you know?'

Abby turned to Max. 'Can you believe she said that about us?'

Max shrugged. 'It got us out of a hole,' he said. 'I think it was pretty smart.'

'So she's the smart one and I'm the simple one, is that what you're saying?'

'You know it's not,' Max told her. 'Come on, the others are up there. Let's get moving.' He pushed past the arguing girls and crossed the street. Lukas and Sami were still loitering at the corner, waiting to turn left down a side road. Their eyes were questioning as Max, Abby and Lili re-joined them.

'What's going on?' Lukas demanded.

'Ah, nothing,' said Abby. 'Just Lili telling everybody that me and Max are stupid.'

'What?' Sami asked.

'Never mind,' Max said. 'Look.'

He gestured down the side road. This was the route they had intended to take towards Blue Command territory. But right now it was blocked by a black armoured vehicle that took up almost the entire width of the road. It had high, heavy bumpers and a small, square windscreen. Its headlights were on but it wasn't moving. It merely blocked the way,

54

like a huge, immovable guard dog. None of the locals were venturing down that street.

'It's the BOPE,' Lukas said.

'Looks to me like they're protecting Blue Command territory,' Abby said. Her outrage at Lili had already subsided.

'So what do we do?' Sami said.

Max consulted his mental image of the favela map. 'We find another way in,' he said. 'Follow me.'

7

Turf War

It was almost dark as the cadets continued uphill, past a barber's, a tyre shop and another mini-mart. The houses on either side were more run down than those they'd passed earlier: they had bare breezeblocks, rotten window frames and broken panes. Roofs had buckled. Walls were stained around the downpipes, and the smell was even fouler than before. A scrawny dog chewed on a half-eaten chunk of meat. Motorbikes buzzed up and down the road.

Max led them away to the left. There were far fewer people here, even though the road was wide. A small group of children kicked a football around, dodging the litter strewn over the ground. As the cadets watched them, there were several bursts of gunfire in the distance. The children scattered, disappearing into the buildings on either side.

'How far away do you think that was?' Abby said.

'Two hundred metres, maybe a little more,' Sami said

confidently. Having experienced urban gunfire in Syria during the civil war, he was able to make that judgement.

Max peered down the street. He could see that at the far end, it was blocked. Squinting, he could make out a solid barrier at least three metres high. It had holes here and there. 'To shoot through,' Lukas said.

'I think there's some kind of door in the middle of the barrier,' Max said. 'I guess they only let people they recognise into that part of the favela.'

'Well, they're not going to recognise us,' Lukas said. 'We need to find another way in.'

Max frowned. 'I don't know,' he said. 'I think all the access roads into Blue Command territory are going to be blocked in some way. I'd rather risk a roadblock guarded by some low-level gang members than by the BOPE.' He turned to the others. 'What do you all think? Shall we take a closer look? As there's a solid barrier, there may not even be anyone guarding it. If there is, perhaps we can distract them.'

'That's what I like about you, Max,' Abby said. 'Your blind optimism.' She started walking down the street then looked back over her shoulder. 'So are you all coming, or what?'

They kept to the pavement on the left-hand side. There were no street lights so they were able to stay in the shadows. They moved in single file – Abby first, then Max, Lukas, Sami and Lili. It was immediately obvious that this street led to a dangerous area. There were no shops or cafes. No pedestrians. House windows were barred, doors were locked. There was a riot of graffiti on the walls and the cadets had to move around an enormous pile of litter that had accumulated on the pavement. There were plastic bags of rotten rubbish and even an old fridge, dented and half-open, lying on its side. Max thought he saw the movement of rodents among the debris.

They were a quarter of a football pitch from the barrier when Abby held up a hand. They were by a house whose first floor had a precarious overhang. It looked like it could collapse at any minute, but it afforded them good cover from which to survey the barrier. It was constructed from breezeblocks. A vicious roll of razor wire lay along the top. Max counted five gun holes and it looked to him as if the door could only be opened from the other side.

'I don't see how we can get through that,' Lili said. 'Even if we manage to create a distraction, we can't climb over –'

She didn't finish her sentence, because there was a sudden noise behind them.

Max looked over his shoulder. Movement. A small crowd was approaching from the way they'd come. He estimated that there were fifteen people, and they were running, rather chaotically, in the cadets' direction. They were young – very young, some of them. Aged between seven and sixteen, he reckoned. And many of them – all of them, perhaps – were armed. Some of the younger kids held handguns in the air, and they were shouting excitedly.

'Get down!' Lukas said. As one, the cadets crouched behind the sprawling pile of rubbish. The newcomers were still running their way and Max could see now that they all wore bandanas over their faces. Not blue bandanas, like he would have expected of Blue Command gang members. These were a mixture of reds and dirty oranges, covering their noses and mouths, but not their eyes, which gleamed with a wild ferocity.

'It's a different gang,' Lili whispered.

'Turf war,' Lukas said. 'They want to grab some of Blue Command's territory and they're going to fight them for it. This is going to get noisy.'

The gang had moved past the cadets' position now. Either they had not seen the five of them crouching in the shadows behind the litter pile, or they had chosen to ignore them. They were about ten metres closer to the barrier when they stopped. The cadets watched them from behind. They formed a single line across the road. The excitement of the younger ones had suddenly seemed to evaporate. They were quiet and still. He couldn't see their firearms, but from the way some had their arms raised, others their shoulder hunched, he reckoned that ten of the youngsters had pistols while five had something more powerful. Submachine guns, perhaps.

'They're going to be massacred,' Sami whispered. 'Standing in a line like that, one burst of fire from the barricade will take them out.'

He was right. The kids in the red bandanas might be armed and keen, but they were no military tacticians.

'Get flat on the ground,' Max urged the others. 'There's going to be crossfire, ricochets . . .'

One of the gang members shouted an instruction. There was suddenly a thunderous cacophony as fifteen weapons fired towards the barrier. Lumps of concrete and clouds of dust burst from it. Max pressed himself hard to the ground, covering his head with his hands.

Silence.

Any minute now, he told himself, the people behind the barrier would shoot back. They would be aiming for the gang, but there was nothing to stop loose bullets heading towards the cadets. 'Keep low!' he whispered. '*Keep low!*'

Ten seconds passed.

Twenty.

There was no retaliation.

One of the younger kids shouted something and laughed. He raised his arm, pointed his handgun to the sky, and fired. There was a muzzle flash and the retort echoed against the buildings. Two more kids laughed, and the line of armed youngsters started to move closer to the barrier.

'We should leave,' Lili whispered. 'Go back the way we came. Get out of –' She was looking back along the street as she spoke. 'Oh no!'

All the other cadets had been focused on the line of youngsters. Now they followed Lili's gaze. Max's stomach lurched. A vehicle was visible at the end of the street. It was no ordinary vehicle. It was one of the armoured vans they had seen minutes previously. Perhaps it was even the same one. It was moving slowly towards them, its engine low and grumbling.

'BOPE,' Max said.

Abby looked at the barrier, then at the armoured van, then at the barrier again. 'We're trapped,' she said, a hint of panic in her voice. She swallowed hard. 'We have to get past the vehicle before any of those BOPE guys get out. Remember what Hector said: some of them are on Blue Command's side. They're going to open up on this lot and we're going to get caught in the middle!'

The cadets didn't need telling twice. They jumped up from their prone position. At the same time, Max saw a couple of the gang members turn around. Their eyes widened and they shouted out in alarm.

'*Run!*' Max bellowed.

The cadets raced back up the street. But they didn't get far. The armoured van had stopped. Behind the glare of its headlights, Max could see figures emerging from the vehicle. Eight, maybe more. He could see their weapons and the smooth outline of their heads – they were wearing balaclavas. Four of them had ballistic riot shields. They positioned themselves efficiently in a line in front of the armoured van, kneeling down behind the shields. The van's headlights cast long shadows along the road, almost reaching the group of young gunmen, who appeared disorderly in comparison. They were shouting at each other, a couple of the older boys waving their arms around and shouting instructions at the younger ones. Two of them discharged their weapons into the air, but it seemed to have no effect on the armed police. The four officers who had no riot shields took up position behind those who did. A voice came over a loudspeaker from the armoured vehicle. Max couldn't understand the words but he understood their meaning. *Put down your weapons!*

It was never going to happen. One of the older gang members aimed his submachine gun towards the armed police and opened fire.

It was a five-second burst, with a bright orange muzzle flash from the barrel of the weapon. Max was used to the sound of an MP5 from his time on the range, but still, the noise was nasty. Bullets hit the ballistic shields, and a few ricocheted off the armoured vehicle. Instinctively, the cadets hit the ground again. Neither of the two sets of combatants seemed to have noticed them. Or if they had, they plainly didn't care that they might get hit in the crossfire.

There was an awful moment of silence. Then the armed police retaliated.

Max and the other cadets had been well trained in the use of firearms. They were adept with pistols, submachine guns and rifles. But it was one thing handling weapons on the range. Being in the middle of a blazing firefight was quite another. The four BOPE guys without riot shields stood up and stepped to the right. It was a choreographed move. Max was weirdly reminded of books he'd read when he was younger that showed Roman legionaries attacking from behind a wall of shields. Unlike Roman legionaries, however, the BOPE were equipped with automatic weapons and laser sights. Each of the four men aimed their weapons with quick precision. Max glanced at the gang members. Red dots danced on the chests of the four biggest. The four police weapons fired a single shot. The four gang members crumpled to the ground. Quickly, the police marksmen positioned themselves back behind the ballistic shields.

The sudden death of four of their members had an immediate effect on the gang. They scattered from the middle of the street towards the pavements. Several of them fired handguns uselessly towards the armed police. They were young, and their weapon-handling skills were poor. Bullets slammed into the building behind the cadets.

'Is anyone hit?' Max shouted.

'We're fine!' Sami yelled. 'But we have to get out of here!'

Easier said than done. They were sandwiched between two warring parties. The gang members had mostly taken up defensive positions. Some were hiding behind a car parked on one side of the road. A couple were in a doorway. One or two were lying behind another pile of rubbish close to the barricade. They were taking occasional and ineffective potshots at the armed police, who were slowly moving forward, protected by their ballistic shields, their armoured van trundling along behind them.

The shots from the gang members became more frequent. They were getting desperate, yelling at each other in panic, and their aim was getting wilder. Stray bullets flew more frequently over the cadets' heads and into the wall behind them. The BOPE personnel and their armoured van halted. The occasional bullet pinged off their ballistic shields, but it was clear that gang members had no chance of harming them, and every chance of being massacred.

Opposite their position, on the other side of the street, a door opened.

The door was set back from the dilapidated facade of the house. An old woman appeared. Her shoulders were stooped, her face lined and leathery. She made an urgent gesture to the cadets, encouraging them into her house and away from the gunfire.

Max looked left and right. The armed police were preparing to fire again. The rate of gunfire from the gang members was increasing. Anxious sweat dripped into Max's eyes. The old woman gestured again.

'We can't!' Lukas shouted. 'We can't cross the road! We'll get hit!'

He was right. At the moment, the combatants were not focusing on the cadets. But if they ran across the road, the BOPE would surely mistake them for gang members . . .

'We have to get out of here!' Sami said. 'That last bullet nearly hit Max. If we don't do something, we're dead.'

'Flashbangs!' Abby said. She took off her rucksack and yanked out one of the canister-shaped grenades the Watchers had given them. The others did the same. 'Me, Max, Lukas,' Abby said, 'we'll throw ours at the police. Sami and Lili, chuck yours at the kids. As soon as they go off, we run. Agreed?'

'Agreed,' the others said.

'OK. On the count of three. One . . .'

Max gripped his flashbang and tucked one finger into the loop of the pin. He rolled over so he was facing the armoured van and the police.

'Two . . .'

He swore under his breath. Another armed police officer had emerged from the van. He was standing by it, protected from the gunfire by his police colleagues and by the van itself.

Like the others, he wore a balaclava, but his was slightly different. On the forehead there was a silver insignia of some sort. Max couldn't make out the detail – and in any case, he had more important things to worry about. The police officer raised his assault rifle – and it was not aimed at the gang members. It was aimed at the cadets.

'Three . . .'

Max looked down at his body. A red dot danced on his chest. He shuffled back. The red dot appeared on the pavement, then moved back up to his chest.

'*NOW!*'

Max didn't hesitate. He pulled the pin on his flashbang grenade and hurled it as hard as he could at the police officer with the silver insignia on his balaclava. The others threw their grenades at the same time, and the flashbangs clattered to the ground: two in the middle of the road just in front of the barrier; two in front of the line of riot shields; one in front of Max's marksman.

There was a moment of silence.

Then they exploded.

The noise was ear-splitting. Even Max, who was expecting it, found himself momentarily disorientated. He had his eyes clenched shut to protect them from the sequence of bright flashes that he knew would accompany the sound, but could see the flashes through his closed eyelids.

'*Go!*' Abby shouted. '*GO!*'

Max opened his eyes and pushed himself to his feet. The other cadets did the same. In his peripheral vision, he could see the BOPE guys with their arms over their eyes. He raced across the road. The old lady was no longer visible, but the door was still open. Every cell in Max's body urged him towards it. The others were all around him, sprinting just as fast.

Distance to the other side of the road: fifteen metres.

Ten metres.

Five.

Lukas and Abby were through. They disappeared into the house. Sami was next, hurling himself through the open doorway. Lili moved like a ghost, slipping quietly off the street and into the house.

Which left Max. He was almost at the entrance when he saw the red light on the wall to his right. He threw himself forward, half jumping, half diving. At the same time he heard gunfire. A chunk of brick exploded from the wall just where he'd seen the red dot. Grit showered his face. Some went into his eyes, half blinding him. He clattered into the house, his eyes half shut. Someone grabbed his arms and he heard the door shut behind him. A female voice, elderly, was talking quickly in Portuguese. Max forced himself to open his eyes. They were watering badly, and he had to keep blinking. Abby was holding him, looking concerned. 'You okay?' she said.

'Yeah,' Max replied. 'I think so. That BOPE guy tried to shoot me, but he missed.'

Abby's eyes flashed. It was obvious what she thought about someone trying to shoot her friend. Max looked around. They were in a dingy room, with a single bulb hanging from the ceiling. The only other light came from an old television in one corner. There was no picture: just a blank blue screen, occasionally flickering. Crumbling bare plaster covered the wall, and a few items of old furniture were dotted around. In the middle of the room was a trapdoor with some stairs leading down to a basement. The old lady was holding it open and speaking urgently to them in Portuguese. She was obviously telling them to get down into the basement. To emphasise her point, there was another burst of gunfire outside.

Lukas and Sami were already descending into the basement. Lili said something to the old lady, who replied quickly but ushered her down through the trapdoor as she spoke. Max was still a bit shaky, so he allowed Abby to guide him down the stairs. Within seconds the trapdoor had shut above them, plunging the cadets into darkness.

8

New Best Friend

Lukas was the first to switch on his torch. It glowed red rather than white, because this would preserve their night vision if they had to switch it off suddenly. Max wiped the tears from his gritty eyes. In the dim light, his friends looked scared, and for a moment nobody spoke. Abby switched on her torch, then Sami did the same. There was enough light to see clearly where they were. It wasn't nice.

The roof sagged. Pools of water lay on the floor and rat-like shapes scurried into corners as the light disturbed them. It smelled damp and the brick walls were crumbling. In one of them, however, there was a door. Abby pointed at it. 'Did the old lady tell you where that goes?' she asked Lili.

Lili shook her head. 'She just said that too many children have been killed in the favela. I think she said her kids died. That's why she wanted to help us.'

There was the sound of footsteps up above.

'We can't stay here,' Max said. 'If the police arrive . . .' He couldn't shake the image of the man with the silver insignia on his balaclava – or of the dancing red dot.

The others nodded their agreement. Lukas tried the handle. It was stiff, but it opened with a squeak. He shone his torch through into the next room. 'It's another basement,' he said. 'Just like this one. With another exit.'

'They're connected,' Max said. He ran his hand through his hair and took a moment to work out his bearings. 'If we head that way, the basements will take us past the barrier into Blue Command territory.'

Gunfire was still audible. The cadets entered the next basement, which was indistinguishable from the first: the same sagging ceiling, dilapidated brickwork, wet floor and scurrying rodents. The door on the other side was open. On the far side of the third basement there was no exit, but an opening in the wall and a few old tin cans rusting on the floor. Max wondered if anybody ever came down here. He pointed his torch at the ceiling. There was no sign of a trapdoor here. Maybe the only access was the one they had used. In which case, how were they going to get out?

The cadets crossed another two basements before they came to a brick wall with no exit. In the final basement, however, there was another trapdoor. But there were no steps leading up to it. Lukas and Lili were the tallest of the cadets, so Lili clambered up onto Lukas's shoulders. 'Kill the torches,' she told everybody. 'If I drop the hatch, it's because there's people in the room above. If that happens, run back into the next basement. We can defend ourselves better there.' The cadets switched off their torches, plunging themselves once more into darkness. A dim slice of light appeared as Lili pushed up the trapdoor.

The cadets listened carefully. The gunfire had subsided – or maybe they just couldn't hear it any more. There was no sound from the room above. Lili manoeuvred the hatch to one side, then grabbed the edge of the opening and hauled herself up. She moved out of sight for a moment, then reappeared. 'It's okay,' she said. 'Nobody's here.'

Lukas gave Abby and Sami a leg-up. Once they'd grabbed the edge of the opening, they were strong enough to haul themselves through without difficulty. Max wiped his sore eyes, then approached Lukas.

'You okay?' Lukas asked. 'I thought for a minute they'd put you down.'

'They'll have to try harder than that,' Max said with a grin. He accepted Lukas's leg-up and hauled himself into the room above. Then he leaned back down through the trapdoor, stretching out his hand. Lukas grabbed it and Max pulled him up.

The room was similar to the old lady's. They could hear gunfire again.

'Who do you think lives here?' Sami said.

'I don't know,' Max said. 'Maybe no one.'

There was a broken window on the far wall, beside a door. Max and Abby approached the window and looked out. The house faced a large square. To their left were some metal barricades. Max's sense of direction told him that they were on the far side of the barricade the gang members had been attacking. There was no sign of Blue Command

70

personnel on this side. Maybe they had decided to leave the fighting to the armed police unit. In fact, there was no sign of anybody in the square.

'I guess nobody wanted to stick around when the bullets started to fly,' Abby said.

'Wise decision,' Max said. He examined the square. A few motorbikes were propped up against walls. Cables tangled overhead. The houses surrounding the square were three storeys high. Max didn't like the look of the dark windows on the first and second floors. Anyone could be hiding in the darkness with a weapon. It would be easy to take potshots at anybody entering the square.

Yet the cadets couldn't stay here. They had to keep pressing on, further into Blue Command territory. It was the only way they had a chance of rescuing the ambassador's son – wherever he might be.

Max turned to the others. 'We need to get out of here while the square is empty. But I think we should put on our bandanas. I don't think we'll come under fire immediately if people think we're in Blue Command.'

'That's a big risk,' Lukas said. He jabbed a thumb over his shoulder to indicate the direction of the firefight they'd just escaped. 'Those red-bandana kids? There could be more of them.'

'It's a risk,' Max agreed. 'Anyone got a better plan?'

Nobody spoke.

'Then let's move.'

The cadets removed their scarves and reached into their rucksacks. They pulled out their bandanas and tied them around their faces. It had an instant effect. They all looked suddenly more aggressive and, crucially, anonymous. 'We need to get across the square and down the road on the western side,' Lili said. 'I think that will take us towards the heart of Blue Command territory.'

'When we get outside,' Max said, 'we need to run across the square individually. We don't want to bunch up in a group because that will make us an easier target.' Not for the first time, he wondered when he had started thinking like a military tactician.

The cadets nodded. Abby opened the main door, checked left and right, then sprinted across the square. The other cadets followed: Lili, then Sami and Lukas. Max was the last to go. He stood in the doorway and saw the others congregate on the corner of the street heading west. As Max prepared to join them, something stopped him. Had he seen movement at a first-floor window opposite? He felt suddenly very exposed, reluctant to put himself out in the open.

Then he heard another noise. It came from beneath the room. He ran over to it. Two men were in the basement. They had torches, and weapons, and balaclavas, and body armour. He cursed. Then one of them looked up and saw him standing there.

The trapdoor was propped open. Max kicked it shut. He ran to the door, glancing up at the first-floor window as he burst into the square. There was definitely someone there. Were they a threat? It was impossible to tell. All Max could do was run.

He flew across the square. He didn't travel in a straight

72

line, but zigzagged to make himself a more challenging target, should anybody have him in their sights. He wanted to look back over his shoulder, but he knew that would slow him down, so he kept his eye on the street corner where the other cadets were. Lukas, Sami and Lili were out of sight. Abby was watching him, her face urging him on, one arm outstretched. It occurred to Max that she looked more concerned for his safety than she ever had for her own. When he reached the corner of the street, she grabbed him and hugged him fiercely – and somewhat unexpectedly. Lili stood just behind her. Her brow was sweaty and she seemed out of breath. But there was something in her eyes as she watched the two cadets hugging. Despite the danger, she almost looked amused.

Max unravelled himself from Abby's embrace. He pressed himself against the building at the corner of the street and looked back across the square. He had a full view of this side of the barrier, with its roll of razor wire curled along the top. Someone was desperately trying to claw their way over the barrier. A single shot rang out, and the climber slid back out of view.

There was silence.

Max didn't have long to feel sick about what he'd seen. The door of the house they'd escaped from was still open and a figure stood there. Max instantly recognised him: he had the silver insignia on his balaclava. He was the BOPE guy who had tried to shoot him. Only then did he remember the picture Hector had shown them back at the hotel. It was the Jackal, the BOPE man Guzman paid to keep the police

73

onside! His weapon was slung across his chest and he was looking Max's way. Their eyes met across the square. The Jackal didn't engage his weapon. He must have realised that Max would disappear before he had a chance to take the shot. Instead he raised his right hand and made the shape of a gun with two fingers and a thumb.

Max retreated away from the street corner, out of sight of the BOPE.

'You okay?' Abby asked.

'Yeah,' Max muttered. 'Just making a new best friend, is all.'

'It was only a hug,' Abby said, blushing.

'Yeah. Not really what I meant.' He looked back along the street. It meandered uphill and to the right. Now that the gunfire had stopped, people were emerging from their houses. 'Let's keep moving,' he said quietly.

The cadets pressed on.

9

Pepe's Predicament

Woody and Angel had gone quiet.

They had been staring at the laptop screen in the safe house since the cadets had left. The tiny dots indicating their positions had been glowing on the screen, moving towards Blue Command's territory. They had watched as the cadets split into two groups. Their pulses had risen somewhat when Lili's dot had separated from the leading group and re-joined Max and Abby. They had felt a little calmer as the group moved forward as one.

But now they were grim-faced. Their fingers twitched. The five dots had disappeared.

'What's going on?' Angel whispered. She wanted to get out there and find out for herself, but she was experienced enough to know that she had to accumulate as much intel as possible before making an operational decision.

Woody didn't answer immediately. He was looking at his phone. It was gloomy in the room and his face was bathed in light from the phone and laptop screens. Ten seconds passed in silence. 'We've got a problem,' he said. He showed Angel the screen. It was open on the Fogo Cruzado app. Woody had zoomed in to the Complexo do Alemão, and specifically on the cadets' last known location. He held it up to Angel. The app indicated gunfire in that location, and it was happening right now.

Angel felt the blood draining from her face. She scraped her chair back and stood up.

'Wait,' Woody told her.

'What do you mean, wait? They're in trouble. We have to go in. Get Hector on the phone. Tell him what we're doing.' She cursed under her breath. 'I told him this was madness,' she muttered.

'If they'd been hit,' Woody said, 'their GPS locators would still register.'

'Not if their phones have been taken and destroyed.'

'Okay, but I think they're hiding. We need to give them a couple of minutes. Seriously, Angel, sit down. They're smart kids. Trust them.'

Angel frowned but did as he said. They continued to stare at the laptop. Angel realised they were both holding their breath.

Pepe was not enjoying his game of football. His friends were as noisy as always, yelling at him to pass every time he had the ball. They were in good spirits and full of jokes. But Pepe couldn't stop thinking about what had happened. What he had done.

He couldn't stop hearing his parents' voices. *You end up paying the penalty.*

He knew he'd made a big mistake.

His first instinct had been to pretend he hadn't done anything wrong. He could always deny having spoken to those Blue Command boys. Nobody else had seen him do it, he thought. It was like the time he had stolen a fidget spinner from a shop and pretended he'd found it in the street. Nobody could prove otherwise. But as he tried to dribble the football past one of his friends, and was easily tackled because he was so distracted, he realised this was different to the fidget spinner. Nobody had got hurt then. Now, however, his family might be in danger – because of him.

He had to do something about it.

'I've got to go,' he told the others. The other team had just scored and were hugging each other like they saw real footballers do on the TV – when the TV was working.

His friends frowned, then they looked at the leather football. Pepe grabbed it. 'It's okay,' he said. 'I'll be back tomorrow.'

Without waiting for a reply, he turned his back on them and ran, clutching his precious football to his chest.

The evening was warm and the favela streets were crowded and noisy. It didn't matter to Pepe, who knew these maze-like roads and alleys as well as he knew his own face. He cut through the crowds and across the traffic with speed. It only took five minutes to arrive at the top of the street where he lived.

There he stopped. He was almost sick.

A police vehicle had parked just beyond the alleyway that led to the entrance to his house. Armed officers with their trademark balaclavas had emerged. Breathless, his heart pumping and his skin tingling, he watched five of them disappear down the alleyway while another stood guard at the front.

He knew that they had come for his family.

The penalty.

For a moment he was paralysed. He had to warn them. But there was no way of getting into the house. Not now the death squad had arrived.

Pepe was small and he was sometimes naughty. But he was sharp and quick. He could see that the first-floor window of the house was open. Maybe, he thought, he could shout at them from the window opposite, the one above the cafe. He was good at slipping into places unseen, after all.

He sprinted down the street.

There was still no sign of the cadets on the laptop screen.

A minute passed.

Two minutes.

Both Watchers exhaled suddenly. Five dots had reappeared on the screen. The cadets had changed position. They seemed to be in a house in a square on the edge of Blue Command territory. Angel threw her head back in relief.

And then she saw the sniper.

Angel and Woody faced an open window, which meant they could see across the street to the first floor of the cafe opposite. There was another open window there. The room beyond it was in near-darkness. But Angel could just make out the silhouette of a gunman hunched behind it, a weapon pressed into his shoulder.

She looked down and saw the tiny red dot of a laser sight. It was not on her chest. It was on Woody's.

The cafe was even busier than usual. Lots of people had crammed inside because armed police had arrived in the street and nobody wanted to be close to them. A stressed-out waiter shouted above the noise: anybody who didn't want to buy something should leave. Everyone ignored him, and they certainly paid no attention to Pepe as he squeezed through the crowd. He had been into this cafe many times before and he knew that the door at the back, next to the toilets, led to the first floor. He opened it, unnoticed. He was in a shabby corridor. To the left, the kitchens. To the right, the staircase. He ran up the stairs, two at a time, to a ramshackle landing. The stairs continued upwards, but at the end of the landing a door opened onto the room at the front.

Pepe stared, his mouth agape, holding his football to his chest. A figure was at the window. It was a gunman, crouched and hunched, ready to fire at *his* house!

He wanted to do something. To distract the gunman. To stop him from firing. But he was too shocked and scared. All he could do was stand there and stare.

His body jolted as the gunman fired a single shot.

There was no time to warn him. Angel flung out her left

arm so that it connected sharply with Woody's chest. Then she pushed herself and Woody backwards. Their chairs fell over. At the same time, a shot rang out. Angel's sudden movement must have distracted the sniper. His bullet flew through the window and smashed through the laptop screen before flying across the room and slamming into the wall. Bits of plastic and screen burst into the air, but Woody and Angel were already rolling off their chairs and removing their 9mm pistols from their chest holsters.

'How the hell does anyone know we're here?' Woody demanded. Then he immediately answered his own question. 'Pepe. Has he come back?'

'No,' Angel said. 'The rest of the family are upstairs.'

'They're dead,' Woody said. 'Unless we can get them out of here.'

'That sniper's not on his own,' Angel said. 'There'll be armed men at the entrance.'

'Do we fight back?'

'We don't know what we're up against,' Angel said. 'Hold them back.' She nodded at the stairs leading to the floor above. 'I'm going up.'

Pepe didn't know what to do. His eyes had filled with tears. Who had the man shot? Was his family okay?

You end up paying the penalty.

The gunman didn't move. Perhaps, Pepe thought, he should run up and dislodge him from his position, to stop him shooting again. But he was too scared. He wanted to cry. He wanted to run. He wanted to be anywhere but here.

Most of all, he wanted his mum.

He turned and was about to run downstairs again when he heard shouting from the ground floor. In his panic, he headed back upstairs, his feet making almost no noise. He burst through a door at the top of the stairs and found himself on the roof of the building, next to a blue plastic rainwater collector. He was alone. He could see across the street to the roof of his own house. There was a small ledge at the front. Not knowing what else to do, Pepe crouched down behind the ledge and made himself as small as possible.

He started to cry.

Woody moved over to the entrance, brandishing his weapon in both hands. As Angel ran to the stairs, he kicked the door open and released two rounds in quick succession: a warning to anyone outside. He knelt on one knee in the firing position as Angel raced up the stairs. She burst into the second-floor room. There was one double bed here and three single mattresses. Manuel was lifting one of the mattresses, clearly about to cover the door with it. Marta, Leonardo and Verissimo huddled on the bed, their faces a picture of terror.

'What is happening?' Manuel demanded.

Angel didn't answer. She was too busy looking around the room. There were no windows here. No other exits. Then she looked up. There was a hatch in the ceiling above the bed. It had a small ring pull on it. 'Does that open out onto the roof?' she said.

'Yes,' Manuel said.

Angel jumped onto the bed and yanked open the hatch. Grit and plaster fell from the ceiling, but Angel could see the open sky and the emerging stars. 'Tell your family to let me help them up there,' Angel instructed.

Manuel nodded and started speaking urgent, panicked Portuguese. His wife and children said nothing. They were clearly too scared. Angel grabbed Verissimo first, pulling her roughly up by her arm. There was no time to lose. Once the girl was on her feet, Angel knelt down, wrapped her arms around her knees and lifted her as high as she could. Verissimo grabbed the edge of the opening and struggled through onto the roof. Angel immediately turned to Leonardo. He was heavier, but Angel was strong and fit and easily able to lift him through the hatch to the roof.

Marta was crying. Then there was the sound of gunfire from downstairs. Her sobs became more intense. Angel felt a surge of panic. She could tell from the sound – a burst of fire rather than single pistol shots – that the gunfire had not been Woody's. He was under attack. She hauled Marta to her feet and lifted her up through the hatch, where her children helped to pull her onto the roof.

Which left Manuel. He was a big guy, but Angel didn't blink. As another burst of fire exploded below them, she gestured at him to get on the bed. He did as he was told and allowed her to grab his legs and push him up. Angel was sweating badly and she had to use all her strength, but she managed to get him up through the hatch. She ran to the door and called down to Woody. 'We can exit by the roof!'

'Roger that!' Woody shouted. Angel heard him fire a couple of shots. 'I'm on my way!'

Angel dashed back to the bed. Manuel was leaning over the hatch. His face was sweating and alarmed. 'Come!' he said 'Quickly.' He held out an arm. Angel jumped, grabbed it and allowed him to pull her up onto the roof.

Breathlessly, she took in her surroundings. It was a flat roof with a large puddle in one corner. The building was joined to another on one side, and there was a gap where the alley they'd used to enter separated them from the building on the other side. To jump over that gap would be too risky, because there might be gunmen below. The back wall was separated from the building behind by a much larger gap. Too far, and anyway, Angel knew if she looked down, she would see the courtyard by which they'd entered.

There was only one option. Behind the adjoining building was another roof, a few metres lower. To get to it meant jumping a metre, but that was manageable. From that roof the family could get to several other buildings, and maybe find a way down. Angel pointed at it. 'Take your family that way,' she told Manuel. 'Don't stop, don't look back – get out of the favela if you can. Go to the British Consulate. They'll keep you safe.'

'What about Pepe?'

'We'll find him, I swear to you.'

'What about you?' Manuel asked. His face was wet with sweat.

'I'll follow. I need to get my friend. Go! *Now!*'

Even as she spoke, there was another burst of fire from down below. Angel turned her back on the others and threw herself back into the building, landing expertly on the bed and almost bouncing over to the staircase that led down to the main room. She pulled her weapon, cocked it and took a couple of deep breaths to calm her racing pulse.

Then she headed down.

Pepe's face was wet with tears. His body was shaking. He didn't even dare to lift his face because he was scared of what he might see. He knew the gunfire was coming from his house. Terrible thoughts crossed his mind. His family, dead.

Then he heard a voice. A woman's voice. He recognised it. 'Go! *Now!*'

Gingerly, Pepe raised his head and looked over the ledge. His eyes widened. He could see his mum and dad, his brother and sister. They were on the roof of their house and the English woman who had arrived earlier, the one with the red hair, was urging them to escape across the rooftops. Pepe wanted to shout out to his family, but something stopped him. If he did that, they might delay their escape, and the armed police in the street might hear and see him. So he kept quiet, and watched.

The English woman disappeared. Pepe knew she must have jumped down the hatch into the bedroom. He watched his family move to the next roof along and then jump to the building behind and out of sight. He was trembling and breathless, and had no idea what to do.

At the bottom of the staircase, Angel stopped. Everything was quiet. No gunfire. No voices. Angel raised her weapon and moved her finger from the trigger guard to the trigger.

She turned silently into the room, ready to use her sharpshooting skills to fire quickly on any enemy target that presented themselves.

She froze.

Woody was face down on the floor. His hands were on the back of his head. Two armed policemen in body armour and balaclavas were pointing assault rifles at him. Three more police officers, similarly dressed, aimed their weapons at Angel.

Nobody moved. Angel's handgun remained engaged. But she knew it was hopeless. Even if she took out one of the police officers, the others would shoot her.

Very slowly, she lowered her weapon, uncocked it and laid it on the floor in front of her. She kicked it further into the room, then raised her hands.

The officers were rough. Two of them grabbed her and threw her to the floor. A third ran past her, up the stairs and into the second-floor room. Angel prayed that the family had escaped. The officer returned in less than thirty seconds. He spoke to the others, shaking his head, and Angel knew that, for now at least, the family were safe.

Unlike the Watchers.

Angel felt the barrel of an assault rifle against the back of her head. A knee in the small of her back. Rough hands grabbed her wrists and bound them with plastic cable ties, pulling so tightly that she could feel the blood throbbing in her veins. The same hands grabbed her hair and dragged her to her feet. Woody was already standing. His face was a mess. A swollen cheek. A split lip. A black eye. Blood dripped from one nostril. None of this seemed to bother him. He raised an inquisitive eyebrow at Angel. She understood what he was asking: are the family safe? She nodded. Relief flooded over his bruised and battered face.

One of the police officers collected up the remains of the laptop, but it was useless. The bullet from the sniper rifle had destroyed it completely. Woody and Angel were roughly ushered to the exit. At the top of the external staircase, Angel felt a boot in the small of her back and tripped. She barely managed to remain on her feet. They were forced back down the alleyway, where they could see the flashing neon lights of a police vehicle. The armed officers forced them into the street. The police car – a black SUV with tinted glass and heavy bumpers – was parked in the middle of the road, its doors open and its lights flashing. There were perhaps fifty or sixty people watching from a safe distance, but they looked ready to run if the situation deteriorated.

The police bundled Angel and Woody into the back of the SUV. One officer took the wheel. Two sat either side of the prisoners. The remaining two marched up to the crowd and bellowed at them to disperse.

Woody and Angel remained silent. They couldn't be sure that their captors didn't speak English, and it was important not to say anything that would compromise the cadets or their operation. Angel thought fast. They had been captured by the BOPE, who they knew were in the pay of Blue Command. And if Blue Command knew about Woody and Angel, there was a high chance they knew about Max, Sami, Abby, Lili and

Lukas. Woody and Angel knew that the cadets had always been walking into danger. Now that danger had increased tenfold.

Angel evaluated their options. Could they attack their guards? No. The guards outnumbered them and were too heavily armed. Could they demand to see the British consul? Again, no. The BOPE were in the pockets of Blue Command. They had broken any number of laws already. They were hardly likely to hand Angel and Woody over to the British authorities on request. She doubted they would even be taken to a genuine police station.

So their prospects – and the cadets' – looked grim.

She glanced at Woody. His stern face suggested he was having similar thoughts.

Angel drew a deep breath and closed her eyes for a moment. When she opened them, the SUV had started to move. Crowds of pedestrians parted up ahead and, in the rear-view mirror, she could see them taking to the street again once the police vehicle was safely out of the way. Nobody wanted to be close to the BOPE.

With one exception.

Angel frowned. A young boy was running after the police car. His hair was dishevelled, his face fierce with concentration. He had a leather football under one arm. She recognised him of course. It was Pepe.

She glanced sidelong at Woody. He nodded almost imperceptibly and Angel knew that he'd seen Pepe too. Their BOPE guards, however, showed no sign of having noticed him.

Why would they? He was just a kid after all.

Angel and Woody sat quietly. The police vehicle continued through the favela.

Pepe followed.

10

Lili's Lie

This part of the favela had a different vibe. The houses still looked like they had been built on top of each other. Their walls were still graffitied and bullet-marked. But it was shabbier and more poverty-stricken. There were more wooden shacks than before, constructed from pallets and sheets of corrugated iron. The piles of debris were more numerous and there was a definite stench of rotting rubbish in the air. They passed streets that were completely overgrown with dense foliage. Hundreds of waste pipes led into the greenery, which smelled so bad that Lili had to hold her breath. There were fewer people here. They congregated in groups of five or six, or walked quickly with their heads down, taking care not to catch anyone's eye. Not all of them wore Blue Command bandanas, but they were almost all young. It was as if adults were banned from the streets – and for the first time, Lili understood why this really was a job for the cadets. With their street-kid clothes and blue bandanas, they attracted little attention.

'People are scared,' Sami said. He was walking alongside her, and spoke quietly. He was right, Lili thought. Faces looked down on the street from first-floor windows, drawing back into the darkness when they caught her eye. Pedestrians crossed the road to avoid them.

'Don't worry,' Sami said with his usual earnestness. 'Woody and Angel know where we are.'

'Hope so,' Lili said. But she didn't say what she was thinking: that they had already been caught in the middle of a fierce firefight and the Watchers were nowhere to be seen.

At the next street corner, a teen with a blue bandana like the cadets' leaned against the wall. His eyes locked with Lili's and he nodded in recognition. Lili nodded confidently in return. The kid became distracted as an older man, very thin and with a pronounced limp, staggered up to him. Some kind of exchange occurred. Max couldn't see exactly what, because the old man had his back to him. 'Drugs,' Lili heard Abby saying to him. They were walking in front of her and Sami.

Was it Lili's imagination, or was Abby spending most of her time with Max? She hoped they weren't getting too close. Surely that could only end badly . . .

Abby's voice was disapproving. 'Where I was brought up, you saw it every day. Never ends well.'

Lili remembered that Abby had been born in a rough Northern Ireland prison.

'I guess that's what Tommy came here for in the first place,' Abby continued.

'Yeah,' Max said. 'I guess.'

In the stress of the firefight, Lili had almost forgotten about the ambassador's son – the reason they were here. They still didn't know where he was, and seemed no closer to finding out.

They turned a corner and stopped. The scene that presented itself almost took Lili's breath away – not with wonder, but with anxiety. They were at the top of a flight of wide concrete steps that led down into a large square. It looked to Lili almost like a pit. It was surrounded by three- and four-storey buildings and was perhaps the width of a football pitch. There were a couple of hundred people there, most the cadets' age, some younger. Loud music pumped from some of the surrounding houses. Three fires burned in metal braziers dotted around the square. The kids were in small groups, and there was a definite air of aggression. Some of them brandished handguns as casually as ordinary teenagers might carry a mobile phone. Many wore Blue Command bandanas. Others didn't, but Lili could tell this would be a dangerous place for the wrong person to enter.

She turned to the others. 'I'm going to go down there and talk to someone,' she said.

'It's not safe,' Max told her.

Lili smiled. 'You don't say. How about we quit the favela and check out the beach, if we want safe?'

'You know what I mean, Lili. What if they get spooked by the fact that they don't recognise you?'

'Look, we need information. We're not going to get it by hanging around and hoping we overhear someone talking about where they're keeping a young British hostage. We need to talk to the right people and I'm the only one of us who speaks the language. It has to be me.'

Nobody could argue with that.

'We should position ourselves around the square,' Lukas said. 'Two of us at either end. If you get into trouble, we'll be there.'

'I'll stick with Max,' Abby said quickly. 'You go with Sami.'

Lukas nodded.

'Wait,' Sami said. 'I don't understand what you're trying to do. Nobody's going to tell you where the ambassador's son is, just because you ask them. They probably don't even know.'

'I've got an idea,' Lili said. She didn't want to tell them what it was, because she was afraid they might try to talk her out of it. 'I'm going to pick someone to talk to. Once I've spoken to them, watch them. They'll leave the square and we need to follow them.'

'Lili –' Abby started to say.

But Lili raised a finger to hush her. Before anybody else could raise an objection, she strode off and hurried down the steps into the square.

'I don't like this,' Lukas said as Lili walked away. 'This whole place is crawling with gang members. Trust me, I know how these people think. They get nervous when they don't recognise someone.'

'We can't go after her now,' Abby said. 'We'll draw too much attention to ourselves.'

92

'She's right,' Max said. 'Let's put ourselves in surveillance positions. Lukas, Sami, you take three o'clock. Me and Abby will take nine o'clock. If Lili looks like she's in trouble, we move in, right?'

The others nodded grimly.

Max and Abby waited while Lukas and Sami moved to the right-hand side of the square, taking care to avoid contact with anyone else. They looked like they were deep in conversation, even arguing. It was a good act, and it stopped anybody else approaching them.

'I guess we should get moving,' Abby said. To Max's surprise, she took his hand.

He gave her an inquisitive look.

'It's good cover,' Abby said. 'People are less likely to interrupt us if they think we're – you know . . .' She blushed.

Max didn't argue. Cover was good, and Abby's hand felt warm in his. They set off across the square. Max was careful to avoid catching anybody's eye. The air throbbed with music and a babble of Portuguese. People were shouting at each other, sometimes amicably, sometimes not. There was a thick herbal smell. Max noticed that quite a few of the youngsters were smoking joints. He held his breath, not wanting to become lightheaded from the smoke.

At the far side of the square was another set of steps. Max and Abby sat about halfway up. Abby nudged close to Max. They could see Lukas and Sami, facing each other and talking animatedly. Nobody was paying them any attention. Max tried to pick out Lili. He couldn't see her among the crowd in the square and felt a sudden pang of panic. Then he caught a glimpse of her face. She was weaving her way through the crowd. Her head was down, but even from a distance Max could tell how alert she was. Like a cat, prowling.

'Look out,' Abby whispered.

Max's attention snapped back to the area around them. Nearby, three people were watching him and Abby. They looked a couple of years younger than Max, though their expressions were curiously old, as if they had seen things children shouldn't see. One of them started walking towards them. The other two followed. Max clocked the bulges under their tops: they were carrying concealed weapons. It was clear to Max that they were going to challenge him and Abby. He was about to stand up so they could move away when Abby grabbed him by the arm, leaned in and pressed her lips to his.

Max's eyes widened in surprise. Abby wrapped her arms around him and held him. Awkwardly, he put his arms around her. As Abby continued what seemed to Max to be turning into a very long kiss, it crossed his mind that this was something the Watchers had not prepared him for. Jumping out of aeroplanes, no problem. Negotiating firefights with live ammunition, fine. Kissing Abby? This was uncharted territory. Frankly, he didn't know what to do.

He glanced to the left. The three youngsters looked curiously embarrassed and, after a few seconds, they dispersed into the crowd. Max glanced back at Abby. Her eyes were closed.

'I, er . . .' Max started to say, but the words came out as gobbledegook because they were still mid-kiss.

94

Abby opened her eyes and pulled away from him. 'Did you say something?' she asked.

'I think they've gone,' Max tried to say, but his voice was squeaky and he had to say it again. 'I think they've gone,' he repeated.

'Oh,' Abby replied. She still had her arms around him and didn't appear to be in a hurry to let go. 'Shame.'

'We should check out what Lili's doing,' Max said.

'I guess,' Abby replied. She unwound her arms. 'Don't take this the wrong way, Max, but there's a bit of room for improvement there. Technique-wise, you know?'

Max blushed furiously, but Abby seemed calm. Focused, even. She nodded towards the centre of the square. 'Look,' she said quietly. 'Lili's talking to someone.'

Every time somebody looked at Lili, she felt as if their gaze was burning her skin. She tried to appear nonchalant. To blend in. It was difficult, not just because of her Chinese features but because she felt as if everybody was looking at her with suspicion. And because she knew that, at some point she would have to make contact with people in the square.

She saw Lukas and Sami. They were pretending to have an in-depth conversation. If their plan was to stop people engaging with them, it seemed to be working. She looked to the other end of the square and saw –

Lili shook her head.

Were Abby and Max kissing? Actually kissing? They were. Max looked kind of awkward, but Abby was really going for it. Despite everything, Lili found herself grinning.

'Hey! Look where you're going!'

Lili instantly refocused. She had almost walked into a group of three teens. They were sitting cross-legged on the ground, two boys and a girl. Each of them wore a Blue Command bandana. The girl and one of the boys were smoking a cigarette. Lili hated the stench of the smoke and the way it caught the back of her throat, but she pretended not to. She didn't apologise for her clumsiness. Instead, she maintained a severe expression. 'Anyone got a cigarette?' she asked.

'No,' said the girl, with a sneer that suggested this was a ridiculous request.

Lili shrugged. She looked around casually. Abby and Max had stopped kissing. Abby looked very relaxed. Max's back was ramrod-straight and he looked shaken up. She turned back to the three gang kids. 'Have you heard the news?' she said.

The kids' expressions didn't change. 'What news?' said the girl.

Lili made a show of assessing them before shaking her head. 'It doesn't matter,' she said. 'Guzman doesn't want people to know. I'll catch you later.'

She started to walk away, but the girl jumped to her feet. 'Wait,' she said. Lili turned to see that the girl was offering her a cigarette.

'Thought you didn't have any,' Lili said.

The girl shrugged.

Coolly, Lili took the cigarette and stashed it behind her ear.

'So?' the girl said.

'So what?'

'So . . . what doesn't Guzman want people to know?'

The girl was asking Lili questions now, rather than the other way around. Lili smiled inwardly. That was exactly the way she wanted it. She was in control of the conversation. Her lie would be much easier to deliver. She tried to sound dismissive. 'You probably don't even know about the British boy,' she said.

Clearly hungry for gossip, the girl nodded. 'Yes,' she said. 'Yes, I do. The one who came to the favela. The one they kidnapped. We heard the older kids talking about it.'

Lili shrugged, as if reluctant to admit that the girl knew what she was talking about. She considered asking the girl if she knew where the hostage was being held, but decided that if *she* started asking the girl questions, the balance of power in this conversation would change. So instead she said, 'I heard they're moving him tonight.' She looked around conspiratorially. 'The cartel,' she said. 'From Mexico. They're flying in by helicopter.'

The girl's eyes widened. This was clearly very juicy gossip. The two boys stood up. They looked as intrigued as the girls.

'Hey,' Lili said. 'Keep it to yourself. Guzman doesn't want it to be common knowledge. I shouldn't have told you.'

'Sure,' said the girl. She held up her fist. Lili clenched hers and they touched knuckles. Then she walked on. Only when she'd gone a safe distance and reached a telegraph pole did she risk looking back. She leaned against the post and watched the boy and two girls. They were deep in conversation. Were they talking about what Lili had just said? Were they, as she had calculated, thrilled by the prospect of seeing a Mexican cartel swoop into the favela to airlift Tommy out? Would they know that Lili had lied to them in an attempt to make them lead the cadets to the place where Tommy was being held?

Lili didn't know the answer to any of these questions. But she knew this: the three gang members were on the move. In a conspiratorial huddle, they walked across the square. She looked over at Lukas and Sami. They were moving too, their conversation still in full flow. She checked on Max and Abby. They were following, hand in hand.

Lili took the cigarette from behind her ear and discreetly crushed it before dropping the remnants on the ground.

Then she followed.

11

Leapfrog

There were techniques to following a target in an urban environment. The cadets understood them well. The Watchers had drilled the rules of surveillance into them until they were almost second nature.

Rule one: stay clear of the target's field of vision. This didn't just mean walking behind your target. It meant anticipating their movements. Were they likely to look left and right when they came to a busy road? What would happen to their field of vision if they turned ninety degrees? Might there be obstacles in your path that could offer you a moment of cover if you needed it?

The streets that the three gang members hurried along, however, were straight and narrow. The cadets had no option but to remain almost directly behind them. Apart from the occasional parked car, there were few obstacles, and most of the houses and shops along the way were closed and locked. Worst of all, the targets were jumpy. They kept stopping and looking back. It made it ten times more difficult to follow them.

Rule two: blend in, and change clothes as often as you can. Surveillance targets were more likely to remember clothes and distinguishing features rather than faces. Change a red T-shirt to a green one, or put on a baseball cap or some sunglasses, and you've effectively given yourself a new identity.

But there was no time to change clothes, even if the cadets had had them. The trio were moving quickly and with purpose. It was everything the cadets could do to keep up with them, let alone take steps to alter their appearance.

Rule three: use windows and mirrors wherever possible. If you can survey someone from behind a shop window, they're unlikely to notice you. Even better, get ahead of them and use the side mirrors of parked cars to watch them. It might breach rule one, but nobody expects to be followed from the front.

Rule three was no good to the cadets. It was dark, there were few shops here and none of them were open. Parked cars were few and far between.

Rule four: carry items that give you an excuse for stopping if the target stops moving. A book, a newspaper, a bag of sweets. If you're standing still but occupied, you don't stand out.

But there was no chance of this. The targets were moving quickly and constantly.

Bottom line: the rules of surveillance were no good to them tonight.

Max had no idea what Lili had said to the three gang members who had hurried from the square and were now leading them deeper into the heart of the favela. All he knew was that they wanted to get somewhere fast. And as the cadets could not employ the usual rules of surveillance, they had to rely on their wits.

It was crucial that the trio didn't look back and see Lili. They would surely recognise her in an instant. And as the cadets couldn't change their appearance, they had to change which of them was the lead surveillance person.

They didn't discuss it. They didn't have to. It was almost as if they were thinking like one being. Max went first. He let go of Abby's hand and strode after the trio as they headed uphill. There were plenty of people here, mostly young, many walking with an aggressive swagger, tinny music blaring from their phones. Max avoided looking at them, and went out of his way to walk around any groups of youths. *Learn to be the Grey Man*, he remembered Hector telling them. *Unremarkable. Instantly forgettable. It will get you further than any amount of military know-how or unarmed combat techniques.*

Bearing this in mind, Max tried to look confident, but not too confident. He kept a safe distance from the targets and took care not to look back over his shoulder, but to trust that the other cadets were following, again at a safe distance. He managed to follow them for four or five minutes before the road suddenly turned left and one of the boys he was following happened to look back. Their eyes met. Did he look suspicious? Did the boy think he was being followed?

Max ignored him and walked straight past the trio, knowing this would stop them from thinking they were being tailed. Up ahead he ducked into a side street. He saw the trio pass and then, a few seconds later, Lukas followed them. There was a twenty-second pause before Abby and Sami walked past. He let them go and joined Lili, who trailed behind them.

The leapfrogging continued. When Lukas was spotted, Sami took over. He managed a full ten minutes before Abby had to take his place. By this time, the trio had reached the top of a hill in the heart of the favela. Here, as if there was some invisible cordon, the crowds melted away. It meant that following would be much more difficult. Fortunately, Abby's stint was not a long one. Two minutes later, the trio came to a halt.

A full moon glowed overhead. The road had turned to the left. Max, Lili, Lukas and Sami peered around the corner. They saw an open-air basketball court with a high perimeter fence. A door in the fence swung open, but nobody was playing basketball. Beyond the court was a concrete building, three storeys high but strangely squat. It was larger than the others the cadets had seen so far in the favela and was in better repair, although the buildings around were in a worse state than any Max had yet seen. To Max, it looked like it might once have been an administrative building. It didn't look like a place where people lived. It was heavily guarded. At the main entrance, which was about thirty metres from where Max stood with Lili, Sami and Lukas, stood four older gang members, maybe in their early twenties, openly carrying assault rifles. The ground-floor windows were boarded up with steel sheets. Along the edge of the flat roof were rolls of razor wire, silhouetted against the moon and the clear, inky sky. To the left, Max could see over the jumbled-up rooftops of the favela. In the distance were the twinkling lights of central Rio. He turned away from them as Lili spoke. 'I think that's where they're holding Tommy,' she said quietly.

It certainly looked likely. Why else would it be so heavily guarded? The three gang members they'd been following were making an effort to keep out of sight of the gunmen. They huddled in the shadows against a wall to the right of the basketball court. It looked to Max as if they had lost their nerve. They seemed to be arguing with each other, very quietly of course. A moment later, they moved further along the wall, down an alleyway and out of sight.

'Maybe they didn't like the look of the guards,' Sami said. 'I don't like the look of them either. I think they will try to kill us if we get too close.'

'You think?' Lukas growled. Trust Sami to say it as it was. 'What's Abby doing?'

Unlike the trio, Abby was making no attempt to remain hidden. She was on the far side of the basketball court, by the perimeter fence. She had bent down, ostensibly to tie her shoelaces. But it was clear to Max that she was checking out the guards. The guards had noticed her. How could they not? A couple of them were talking to each other and looking over at Abby. But they didn't seem to be too concerned by her presence: a teenager, and a girl to boot. They turned away and went back to guarding their posts.

Max, though, knew better. When he looked closer, he could see that Abby was not tying her shoelaces. She was groping for something on the ground. She looked back over her shoulder, caught his eye and nodded.

'She's about to do something,' Max said.

'She is going to put herself in danger,' Sami agreed.

Max felt a surge of anxiety at the thought, but Lili didn't allow them time to worry. She grabbed him by the wrist and yanked him back the way they'd come. 'Follow me,' she told the others. 'Quickly!'

Max just had time to see what Abby was doing. She was standing up and her arm had swung back, ready to throw something, Max didn't know what. A stone, probably. But he saw it fly through the air and connect sharply with the head of one of the guards. Abby had a second stone. She threw it. It just missed a second guard. By that time, Abby had turned and was sprinting back to the cadets.

Then Lili had dragged them out of sight. '*Follow me!*' she said. '*Run!*'

There was no time to ask what was going on. It was almost as if Lili and Abby had a telepathic link: one seemed to know what the other was doing. All Max, Sami and Lukas could do was trust them. They ran back down the deserted road and followed Lili as she swung a right down a dark side street. As they turned, Max looked over his shoulder. Abby was running after them.

As soon as they had turned the corner, Lili and the boys stopped. Lili quickly removed her rucksack and pulled a full loop of paracord from it. Suddenly, Max realised what the girls had been planning. Lili unrolled the paracord, took one end and gave the other to Max. They stood on opposite sides of the street and held the paracord taut, about ten centimetres from the ground.

Then Abby came hurtling around the corner. For a second, Max worried that she wasn't aware of the paracord stretched out at ankle height. It was dark, and the cord was difficult to see. But she clearly knew to expect something. Just when Max thought she was going to stumble, she hurtled over the cord like an athlete doing the long jump, then stopped, turned and gestured to Lukas and Sami to join her in the middle of the street. They were facing back the way they'd come when three of the guards came after them.

They were plainly not expecting a trap. They showed no sign of noticing Max and Lili crouching on either side of the street, and they certainly didn't notice the paracord. All their attention seemed to be focused on Abby, and on Sami and Lukas, who were standing either side of her. Their weapons were slung across their chests, but as they ran they raised their rifles into the firing position, preparing to take a shot.

They didn't get the chance.

All three men tripped over the paracord and fell heavily to the ground. In an instant, Abby, Sami and Lukas were on them. They jumped onto the men's backs, preventing them from getting up or accessing their weapons, which were trapped underneath them. Lili was grabbing something else from her rucksack – cable ties to bind their wrists. But as she did that, Abby called, '*Max!*'

He didn't need to reply. He knew what she was warning

105

him about. Only three of the guards had appeared. There was a fourth – probably the guy she had hit in the face with a stone. He was armed, he would be angry, and he could appear around that corner at any minute.

'*Max!*' Abby repeated. He looked over at her. She put one hand in her pocket, pulled out another stone and threw it to him. Max caught it one-handed and ran back up to the corner of the side street. He crouched down, listening hard for footsteps. There was none. Quickly, he took off his bandana, unwrapped it and placed the stone in the centre. He folded the bandana in half, rolled it up, folded it again and held it by the two ends.

He crouched and waited. Back along the street, in his peripheral vision, he could see that Abby had one of the assault rifles and was aiming it at the three gang members while Sami, Lukas and Lili secured their wrists behind their backs. They had the situation under control. Max's job was to put the fourth guy out of action.

He stayed very still and listened very hard. There was still no sound of footsteps. But then, suddenly, he saw a shadow cast by the bright moon. It was long and clear, and it indicated someone approaching the corner where Max was crouching. The person was hugging the wall, and Max could see from the shape of the shadow that he held a weapon engaged in the firing position.

Max held his breath. He could hear the guard's breathing. He estimated that he was immediately around the corner, pressed against the wall like Max was, waiting for his moment to turn and fire.

Five seconds passed.

Ten.

The movement, when it came, was sudden and fast. The guard turned the corner, ready to take a shot. But he clearly wasn't expecting Max to be crouching there. Max wasn't even sure that he'd seen him. Max swung the bandana as hard as he could. The stone slammed against the guard's right kneecap. Max heard it crack first, then the guard's leg buckled. He cried out in pain, but didn't fall. Max saw with horror that the guard still had his weapon engaged and was aiming it at the other cadets.

Max's next move was instinctive. He raised his left hand to push the stock of the weapon so that it was pointing upwards. With his right hand he swung the bandana – even harder this time – against the guard's right knee again.

Three things happened. The guard screamed in agony. He fired a burst of rounds harmlessly into the air, then collapsed to his knees.

Max had a momentary advantage. He dropped the bandana, then stood up and grabbed the stock of the weapon with two hands. He kicked the man in the chest. The man let go of his weapon. Max spun it so the barrel pointed at his adversary. 'Get on the ground,' he said.

The guy probably didn't speak English, but he certainly seemed to understand what Max meant. He glared up at him. For the first time, Max noticed he had a red welt on the side of his face where Abby's stone had hit him. He lay on the ground, face down.

In an instant Lili was there, gripping a cable tie. She

jumped onto the man's back, grabbed his wrists and tied them together. Sweat ran down her face, and Max was breathless. 'What do we do with them?' he whispered urgently.

Lili's expression was steely. 'We take them with us,' she said. 'Try to lock them up somewhere. Otherwise they'll just raise the alarm.'

She stood up and said something in Portuguese to the guy on the ground. He struggled to his feet, unable to keep his eyes off Max, who continued to hold him at gunpoint. Max looked over his shoulder to see that Abby, Sami and Lukas had also confiscated their opponents' weapons and the gang members were groggily standing up. Max's friends urged their captives over to where he and Lili were standing.

'What about these?' Lukas said, indicating the weapons four of them were now carrying. 'Hector said no firearms, remember?'

Lukas was right. But they'd seen the kind of firepower they were up against. 'I don't think we have a choice,' he said.

None of the cadets disagreed.

Lili peered out from the side street, back towards the building the guards had been protecting. 'The coast is clear,' she said. 'We can enter the building if we hurry.'

'Let's move,' Max said. He nudged his captive with the barrel of his weapon.

The Special Forces Cadets advanced to target.

12

Spray and Pray

They moved as a single unit.

Their captives went first, a line of four, hands behind their backs. Lukas was following, holding them at gunpoint. They could not see that he was also checking the first and second storeys of the building to ensure nobody was watching them. Sami and Abby covered left and right, scanning the area on either side of the target building, looking for threats, their fingers resting on the trigger guards as they'd been taught. Max walked backwards, checking for threats behind them.

The three youngsters they'd followed here had disappeared. Clearly being at the centre of Blue Command operations had spooked them. It took the cadets less than a minute to reach the building. Lili, who was unarmed and had been walking in the middle of the group, pushed past their hostages and tried the main door. It was unlocked. A slice of light emerged when she pushed it, but she didn't want to risk entering without a weapon. She looked over at Max and nodded. He joined her, his weapon engaged and pointing at the entrance.

Lili held up three fingers.

Two fingers.

One.

Gently, she kicked the door open. Max stepped in and scanned the room with his rifle. Cracked tiles on the floor. Distressed walls. A strip light overhead. No personnel. Two doors: one to the left, one in the far wall.

'Clear,' he said.

The others hustled their captives inside. Abby quickly headed to the door on their left. She checked the room beyond. 'It's empty,' she told the others. 'We can put them in there.'

Sami and Lukas kept guard while Max, Lili and Abby moved the hostages into the room. Lili bound their legs with cable ties while Max kept them quiet at gunpoint. Once they were secured, Max said to Lili, 'Find out where the hostage is.'

Lili nodded, then spoke to the guards in Portuguese. None of them answered. Max stepped up to the nearest hostage, put one foot on his chest and aimed the weapon at his head. That did the trick. The frightened man gabbled something in reply.

'Second floor,' Lili said. 'Behind some kind of metal door – at least that's what I think he said.'

They left the room and closed the door behind them. Abby crashed the butt of her rifle against the handle. 'They won't get out of there in a hurry to alert anyone,' she said with satisfaction.

Max's attention, though, was already on the far door. He moved stealthily towards it, aware of the others following. When he reached it, he listened hard. There were voices on the other side. They did not sound stressed or alarmed. There was certainly no indication that they realised the building had been infiltrated. But the voices were getting louder. People were approaching.

He tried to determine how many there were. He could clearly identify three, so he held three fingers in the air and stood to one side. Abby, Sami and Lukas knelt in a line facing the door. Lili, unarmed, crouched behind them.

They waited.

When the door opened, the sound of laughter drifted into the room. The three young men who entered were obviously sharing a joke. They were so distracted by it that they failed to react when they saw the cadets. By then it was too late. Max had his weapon pointed at them. The others had them covered from the front. Lili barked an order in Portuguese and they immediately hit the floor. It occurred to Max that they had no way of knowing that the cadets would never use their weapons on them. They were clearly terrified. They didn't even struggle as Lili bound their wrists behind their backs, then tied their ankles together.

'Lukas, watch them,' Max said. Lukas's eyes flashed. He didn't like being told to stay behind. But he nodded and kept his weapon trained on the three men on the ground. Max, Sami, Abby and Lili walked along a corridor. There was a flight of stairs at the end. Max pointed his weapon up it and the others advanced to a half-landing. Max joined them, then covered them as they carried on to the first floor, before following them.

They were in another corridor. It was empty. Another flickering strip light. Ripped linoleum on the floor. Three closed doors were along the left-hand side. The one furthest away was covered by a metal grate bolted to the frame. The grate was locked with a heavy padlock.

Max turned to Abby. If anyone could pick that lock, it was her. 'Can you get it open?' he asked.

She didn't reply. She simply handed Lili her weapon then ran lightly to the end of the corridor, where she removed the cartilage piercing from her ear, shaped it and inserted it into the lock. The others knelt down in the firing position, each covering one of the three doors. Sami took the first, Lili the second, Max the one with the grate. He was right by Abby.

There was silence, broken only by a scratching as Abby tried to pick the lock.

It wasn't opening. She looked over her shoulder at Max, who saw she was sweating. He gave her what he hoped was an encouraging look, then felt foolish as she had already turned back to concentrate on the lock.

Thirty seconds passed.

The padlock clicked open.

Max found himself holding his breath.

Abby opened the grate. Max winced as its hinges squeaked. He glanced back at Sami and Lili, checking that the noise had not disturbed anyone in the other rooms. They were both still in position, motionless and apparently calm.

Once the grate was open, Abby put one hand to the door and gave Max an inquisitive look. With his weapon still engaged, Max nodded.

Slowly, quietly, Abby turned the handle and opened the door a crack. She had one finger to her lips, ready to warn the occupant of the room to keep as quiet as possible.

Then she jumped back.

The door had been yanked open on the other side and a high-pitched, aggressive scream emerged from the room. A figure burst out. He was tall and gangly. He had a cut on one cheek and a swollen black eye. His mouth was open, mid-yell. His eyes were wide, his bleached blond hair dishevelled. Max recognised Tommy, but he looked a lot less suave than he had in his photograph. He threw himself at Abby. Max was reminded of a feral cat throwing itself at a mouse, except this mouse was trained in unarmed combat. In one swift movement, Abby flung him over her shoulder. He landed flat on his back with a heavy thump.

Suddenly silent, he looked up at her. He turned his head to stare at Max. Then back at Abby.

Then he screamed again, like a maniac.

'*Shut him up!*' Max hissed. But Abby was already leaning down and pressing a hand over his mouth to stifle his scream.

It was too late.

There was activity in the other rooms. Voices shouting. Movement. Lili and Sami looked at each other. They nodded. Then each of them raised their weapons so that they were pointing just above their respective doorways. Max braced himself for the deafening sound of gunfire.

113

Sami and Lili fired in unison. Bullets ripped into the area above the lintels, throwing out a shower of debris. At the same time, Max and Abby pulled the boy to his feet. He struggled madly.

'We're getting you out of here,' Max said.

'Who are you?'

'It doesn't matter. Stop struggling and do what we say!'

'How do I know you're really here to help?'

'We're speaking English, aren't we? Which I'm guessing is more than you can say for whoever gave you that black eye. So what do you say? You want to stay with the people who've been roughing you up, or take your chances with us?'

There was another sudden burst of shouting from the other rooms.

'Tell you what,' Abby said. 'Don't answer that. Just shut up and run.' She took him by his right arm and dragged him back along the corridor, past Sami and Lili who still had their weapons pointed at the doors.

'*Go!*' Max urged them.

They didn't have time to move before there was another burst of gunfire. This time, it came from inside the second room. The door splintered and bullets flew just above Sami's head and embedded themselves in the wall behind him. Sami quickly rolled away, out of the line of fire, then released another burst of rounds above the door. Max knew it would only suppress the gunfire from within for a couple of seconds. He hurled himself back down the corridor, past the splintered door, Sami scampering behind. The four cadets and Tommy made it to the stairwell at the end of the corridor just as the second door opened.

'Get downstairs!' Max shouted. 'They're coming out!'

And they were. Three of them at least. In the moment before Max threw himself after the others down the stairs, he saw two Brazilian guys with bare chests, Blue Command bandanas and bandoliers of ammunition strapped around them. The third guy was fully dressed. He had very dark skin, wild hair, a tropical shirt and a chunky gold necklace. Max instantly recognised him as Guzman, the leader of Blue Command. He also recognised the Uzi 9mm submachine gun he carried in one hand. Max saw him raise the weapon, but he was charging down the stairs by the time Guzman opened fire. Max remembered Hector referring to the Uzi as a 'spray and pray' weapon: fiendishly dangerous at close quarters. He heard the gritty, machine-like sound of the weapon firing, and the ricochet of bullets pinging off the walls. Then he heard the heavy thump of footsteps as Guzman and his people sprinted down the corridor.

'*RUN!*' he barked. '*THEY'RE COMING!*'

The cadets took the rest of the stairs three or four at a time. Somehow, Abby managed to keep hold of Tommy. He was so gangly he looked like he might collapse in a heap, but she kept him upright as they descended.

Guzman and his guys were at the top of the stairwell. As the others carried on down, Max pressed his back against the wall of the half-landing and fired upwards. It was suppressive fire, not calculated to hit anyone, but to stop the enemy advancing and hopefully would buy them a few more seconds.

Then he hurried after the others, followed by the sound of Guzman's Uzi coughing out rounds at an alarming rate. The weapon sounded much closer than Max expected.

The four cadets and Tommy burst out of the stairwell onto the ground floor. Lukas was still there, guarding the three guys on the ground. He looked stressed. 'Sirens,' he said curtly. And over their footsteps and his panicked breathing, Max could indeed hear police sirens outside. He swore under his breath.

'We have to get out of here,' Sami said. Nobody argued. Staying in the building wasn't an option. They had to flee into the streets of the favela, even if it meant risking coming into contact with the BOPE.

They ran to the exit, Abby still gripping Tommy. As they exited the building and spilled out onto the street, the source of the siren was immediately obvious. There was an armoured vehicle on the far side of the basketball court. Armed police were jumping out of it, a couple already down on their knees in the firing position.

'This way,' Lukas said. He ran to the left, towards a road leading downhill into the darkness. The others followed. Shots rang out. They ran faster out of the line of fire. Only when the high fence of the basketball court formed a barrier between the cadets and the police did Max dare to look back over his shoulder. Guzman and his guys were running out of the building. Guzman was screaming in anger, waving his weapon. He looked out of control and Max was glad of that: if the gang leader had been thinking calmly, he would surely have sprayed the Uzi in their direction and they'd be dead.

But he didn't, and now they had reached the street. It was deserted. Dark. Anybody with any sense was indoors or far from the area. Max had never run so fast. The others were by his side. Even Tommy, although he looked terrified, managed to keep up. A little way along the road, Lukas dodged into a side alley. At first Max thought it was a massive mistake. It was a dead end and they'd be cornered. But then he saw what Lukas had seen: a metal staircase, like the one that had led up to the first floor of the safe house, only this gave access to the roof of a derelict building. The cadets sprinted up it, Abby urging Tommy to move as fast as possible.

Once they were up the staircase, they pressed themselves down against the roof, bathed in the light of the moon, but unseen from the street. Max's heart thumped. It thumped even harder when he heard men running past below. Rough voices barked instructions. One was louder and more high-pitched than the others. Max wondered if that was Guzman. He crawled to the edge of the roof and looked down at the street. There was a railing that offered some camouflage. He peered down. Sure enough, he saw a group of gang members and BOPE officers below. Eleven men in all, and in the middle of them was Guzman, wild-haired and wild-eyed, waving his Uzi around and screaming angrily at an armed officer in body armour and balaclava. The armed officer stood still, taking Guzman's reprimand without any apparent emotion. Guzman spat on the ground and turned his back on him. The officer turned to face the building and Max clearly saw, on the forehead of his balaclava, the Jackal's silver insignia.

He found himself holding his breath.

Then his blood froze as the BOPE officer looked up.

For a moment, Max thought their eyes met. He did not dare move a muscle. Had the Jackal seen him? He was still looking up at the roof. Then he turned. Max quickly wriggled away from the edge, boiling with the fear that he might have given up their position. He found Sami lying next to him. 'If they find us up here,' he whispered sincerely, 'they will kill us.'

Thanks for pointing that out, buddy, Max thought, but he kept silent.

A minute passed. Guzman's screaming started again, then faded away. Sweating, Max rolled onto his back. 'That,' he said quietly, 'was close.'

'We're not out of the woods yet,' Abby said. Her voice was stressed and tense. None of them dared to stand. 'We need to get to the rooftop of the school and call Hector for the chopper to pick us up. That means getting out of Blue Command territory, and they're going to be looking for us.'

'Roger that,' Max said. 'Maybe we should wait here for a while until Guzman and the BOPE have dispersed.'

'I'm not sure that's a good idea,' said Lili. 'We're too close to their centre of command. This area will be crawling with them very soon.'

'Maybe we should make the distress call,' Sami said. 'I can't see us getting out of here without bumping into them.'

Someone coughed. It was Tommy, reminding them he was there. 'Er, mind if I say something?' he asked. His voice was posh, like his father's.

'Surprised you've got any voice left,' Abby muttered, 'after all that screaming.'

'Ah,' said Tommy. 'Yes. My throat *is* a bit sore. Sorry about that. I thought you were *them*.' He frowned at Lukas. 'Who are you, by the way?'

'We'll explain that when we get the hell out of the favela,' Lukas said.

'Right,' Tommy replied. 'That's what I wanted to talk to you about.' He sat up and ran a hand through his blond hair, which glowed faintly in the moonlight. 'The thing is, I'm not going anywhere. I came here to do something, and I'm not leaving the favela until I've done it.'

The cadets stared at him. Max exhaled slowly. 'Are you crazy?' he said.

13

Seven Minutes, Thirty-Five Seconds

'We're getting out of here,' Lukas said, 'whether you like it or not.'

'That's up to you,' Tommy said. For the first time, there was a hint of steel in his voice. It occurred to Max that the ambassador's son was not quite the person he expected him to be. 'You go. I'm staying. I've got a job to do.'

An aggressive look crossed Lukas's face. 'What, scoring dope on a street corner?'

Tommy looked astonished. 'You think that's why I came to the favela?' he said.

Sami put a hand on Lukas's forearm to stop him replying. Lukas was obviously angry, but he kept quiet.

'I know it sounds crazy, but that's kind of what we were told,' Sami said, smiling. He had a knack of putting people at their ease.

'Who by?' Tommy demanded. 'No, don't tell me. My dad, right? Did he call me a "high-maintenance child"?'

'I think he might have used words like that,' Sami said.

Tommy shook his head in disbelief. 'Since my mum died, that's what he tells everyone. He thinks that if he persuades himself and other people that I'm off the rails, he has an excuse for being in my face all the time. He'll even tell you that I came to the favela to buy drugs, if it means he doesn't have to tell you the truth.'

'What truth?' Lili asked.

'I've come here to find my girlfriend,' Tommy said. 'I've never touched drugs in my life. I'm not an idiot.'

The cadets were silent for a moment. 'Who's your girlfriend, Tommy?' Max said carefully.

'She's called Beatriz,' Tommy said. 'You'd like her!' He scowled, and Max realised this was a boy whose every emotion showed on his face. 'My dad *doesn't* like her. Because she's Brazilian. He . . . he doesn't really like foreigners.'

'Seems to me he's in the wrong job,' Abby observed.

Tommy shrugged. 'It makes him feel powerful. I met Beatriz in a cafe when I was here a few months ago, and we see each other whenever we can. I have to do it in secret, of course. When I told him about Beatriz, Dad banned me from seeing her just because she's poor. But that doesn't matter, does it? She's super-smart, and fun, and –'

'Mate,' Max said, 'we're stuck on a rooftop and surrounded by armed men. I'm sure Beatriz is great, but we haven't got a lot of time. Feel like fast-forwarding a bit?'

Tommy nodded seriously. 'Right. She lives in a different

favela. Not this one – a safer place nearer the centre of Rio. She's kind of well-known because she's such a . . .' Here words seemed to fail him.

'Such a what?' Max pressed.

'Well, a geek, I guess.'

'Nothing wrong with that,' Lili said.

'I know, right?' Tommy said with a big smile. If it wasn't for the bruises and cuts on his face, nobody would know he'd just escaped incarceration. He was like an eager puppy. Then he frowned again. 'Blue Command found out about her. She's amazing with computers, telecoms, all that stuff. And Blue Command have a big problem, don't they? The government have hit their TV networks. Did you know about that?'

'We heard about it,' said Sami.

'Blue Command would pirate the football matches and distribute them around the favela for free, to buy the loyalty of the people who lived in the favela. Easier than taking it by force. But the government cut them off, so they needed somebody who knew how to reconnect them. That's why they took Beatriz. She was easy to abduct and she had all the skills they needed.'

The cadets all looked at Tommy with interest. 'How did you find out about this?' Max asked.

'Her friends saw it happen. They texted me. When I got to the favela I started asking around, which is when I found out about the TV thing. I knew there was no point going to the regular police because they wouldn't dare enter the favela to find someone like Beatriz. So I decided to look for her myself. But someone must have recognised me. They caught me and . . .' He touched his fingertips to his bruised face and winced. 'Guzman's people can be very rough.'

Max was beginning to see Tommy in a new light.

Tommy got to his feet. 'Thank you for your help,' he said. 'I completely understand that you want to get out of here. But I'm going to find Beatriz. I'm not going to leave her to these people. I overheard Guzman talking. I know what he's going to do with her, once she's got his stupid TV network up and running.'

'What?' Lili said. She and Abby suddenly had grim expressions.

'Sell her,' Tommy said.

Sami looked shocked. 'Sell her?' he echoed.

'Right.'

'Like a *slave*?' Outrage emanated from Sami.

Max found himself remembering what Angel had said during their initial briefing. *Blue Command also run a people-trafficking business. They abduct* favelados – *people who live in the favelas – and sell them on to rich families in rural parts of South America.*

'Like a slave,' Tommy confirmed. 'She would be in demand. She's clever, she's competent, she would fetch a good price in other parts of this continent. I'm not going to let it happen.'

'Nor am I,' said Sami quietly.

'Me neither,' said Lili.

'Nor me,' said Abby.

Max and Lukas exchanged a long look. There was no doubt in Max's mind that they were both on Tommy's side, but this was a big call to make.

'Do you know where she is?' Max said.

Tommy nodded. 'I think so. It's not far from here. There's an old warehouse further down the hill. Guzman's people said it's where they broadcast their TV network from. They've locked her in there while she does her engineering. It's probably guarded, but –' he shrugged – 'there *must* be a way of getting her out.'

'It might be safer for her if we waited,' Max said. 'We should get you out of the favela first, then see if we can return with backup.'

'Are you *joking*?' Abby said. The way she looked at him – as if he'd just said the stupidest thing in the world – was a punch in the stomach. 'You think they'd do more for some favela girl than they did for the ambassador's son? Jeez, Max, I thought you were smarter than that.'

Her waspish comment silenced the cadets. Max felt himself blushing, especially when Abby refused to catch his eye.

Tommy broke the silence. 'It has to be tonight, anyway,' he said. 'Guzman said she was nearly finished with the TV thing. They're planning to move her in the morning. Once they get her out of the favela, we'll never find her.'

'You can't do it by yourself,' Max said. He was interrupted by the sound of gunfire. Not close, but not very distant. Tommy blanched, and the cadets frowned.

'If we do this,' Max said, 'we have to break contact with the Watchers. You know Hector would never agree to it.'

The other cadets nodded. They took out their phones and switched them off so that they could no longer be used as tracking devices. 'There's no point waiting,' Abby said. 'Let's do it.'

The gunfire subsided. The cadets crawled across the rooftop back to the metal staircase. One by one, they climbed back down into the street.

Pepe was fit. It was the football that did it. An hour every day, running around with his friends, meant that although he was small and skinny, he could run and run and barely break a sweat. So it had been no trouble keeping up with the police car that had taken the two British people away from his family's house. The difficulty had been staying hidden.

There, his size was an advantage. He could tuck himself into doorways and hide behind cars. He could lose himself in a crowd. And even if he found himself out in the open, he knew he could get by unnoticed because he was a kid. The BOPE police, with their scary weapons and their balaclavas, didn't mind shooting children, but they didn't see them as a threat.

So Pepe not only managed to keep up with the police car, but he also managed to stay unnoticed in the dark. It was a hot night. The BOPE's SUV had parked outside a grim grey building on the edge of the favela. Pepe knew this was the BOPE's local headquarters – and it was a place he should avoid. It was on a busy main road and to one side was a car park full of black SUVs. Pepe watched from the opposite side of the road. The SUV containing the British couple parked at an angle in front of the main entrance. The doors opened and the BOPE men dragged the couple out. The man looked in a bad way. His face was bleeding and bruised. But they weren't resisting. Their heads were bowed, their shoulders sloped. They walked calmly, the armed guards at their side, up the steps that led into the police building, and out of sight.

Pepe stood there for a few minutes once they had disappeared, his brain ticking over. Then, in a gap in the traffic, he crossed the main road and approached the police building.

The secret to being held against your will, Angel knew, was to do as you're told when you have no other option. When your opponents are more heavily armed than you, when they outnumber you two or three to one, you have to play it smart. Be acquiescent. Smile sweetly. Don't make a nuisance of yourself.

Then, when their guard is down and they're least expecting it, you strike.

She allowed herself to be manhandled out of the SUV. Woody did the same. His face was still bleeding and he gave the impression of being easily manoeuvred, like a rag doll. Angel knew that was an act. Woody could take a lot more punishment before he was truly unable to put up a fight.

They were outside a squat grey building by a main road. Angel knew they had to be on the very edge of the favela and she suppressed a surge of anxiety at their distance from the cadets. She looked across the busy main road. Her eyes were dazzled by the car headlights, but she thought she could see the silhouette of a young boy watching them from the other side. She smiled inwardly. He was a persistent one, that Pepe. It occurred to her that he might have the makings of a cadet when he was older. For now, however, she banked the knowledge of his presence. Most adults would dismiss the potential of children in a situation like this. Not Angel. She'd seen what they were capable of.

There were no pleasantries inside the police building. There weren't even any unpleasantries. The BOPE guards dragged them wordlessly across a reception area and down a flight of stairs into the basement. Here they were marched along several corridors until they reached some empty holding cells. The cells were cramped and dirty, each with a toilet in one corner and a hard bed along the back wall. Each cell was constructed from metal bars and had a sturdy lock on the doors. Angel and Woody were thrown into separate cells opposite each other. The cells were locked and the BOPE guards left.

They waited until the guards' footsteps had faded away, then they approached the front wall of their cells. They couldn't be sure that there were no listening devices down here, so they whispered, communicating as much by lip-reading as by speaking.

'Strategy?' Angel asked.

'We've got two options. One, we sit it out. Wait for the cadets to finish their mission. The BOPE will have to release us eventually.'

'I don't like it. Someone informed on us. If they told the BOPE or Blue Command about us, they'll have told them about the cadets. We need to be back in the field in case anything goes wrong.'

'Agreed. Option two – fancy getting the hell out of here?'

'I thought you'd never ask.'

'What do you reckon?' He looked at his watch. 'Ten minutes tops?'

'Ten minutes? You're losing your touch.'

Woody looked offended. 'That's a worst-case scenario.' He looked over his shoulder towards the toilet in the corner of the cell.

Angel raised an eyebrow. 'You want me to turn my back?'

'No. I want you to keep watch.'

Woody stepped over to the toilet. It was unpleasant. There was no seat, and even from a distance Angel could tell that the bowl was dirty. It was an old-fashioned toilet with a high-level cistern on the wall. Hanging from the cistern was a metal chain with a burnished wood handle. Woody stood on the rim of the bowl, lifted the lid of the cistern and felt for the mechanism inside. It was less than a minute's work to remove the chain from the cistern. Holding it, Woody jumped down from the toilet bowl. He held the chain at both ends and tightened it.

'Woody,' Angel said, 'they're not idiots. They'll notice that you've removed the chain from the cistern.'

'Course they will,' Woody said. He walked to the front bars of the cell, checked there was nobody coming, then swung the chain across the gap so that it clattered into Angel's cell. 'I might be wrong,' he said, 'but I think they'll be less vigilant around a woman.'

Angel managed a grin. 'I reckon you're right.' She bent down and picked up the chain, then secreted it under her top, tucking it slightly into her jeans to keep it in place. 'Lie down on the ground,' she said. 'Make it look like you've passed out.'

Woody did as she said. He lay on his side, one hand tucked underneath his body as though he was hiding something. He closed his eyes. It didn't look particularly convincing, but that was the whole point.

Angel started shouting and banging her fists against the railings. '*Hey! Guards! We need help! Get in here!*' There was no response. She carried on shouting. '*We need a doctor! Hey! Can anyone hear me? We need a doctor – now!*'

She heard a door open. A guard approached the cells. He wore the black gear of the BOPE, but now he was safely inside their headquarters, he'd removed his balaclava. He had a couple of days' stubble and a flat nose. He walked with a swagger that suggested he was rather impressed with himself. Good, she thought. That'll make it easier.

He ran his eyes up and down her body.

'He needs a doctor,' she repeated.

The guard didn't say anything. Angel had no way of knowing if he'd even understood what she'd said. He strolled over to Woody's cell. Angel surveyed him carefully. He looked down at Woody, then up at the cistern. He shook his head. Then he turned and sneered at her. He spat something in

Portuguese. Perhaps he was saying, *Do you think I'm stupid?* It didn't matter to Angel, because she was about to use the most powerful weapon she possessed.

Her eyelashes.

Angel was merciless. She fluttered her eyelashes and pouted. The guard didn't stop sneering, but he did saunter over to Angel's cell. Angel gripped the bars with both hands. As he drew nearer, she smiled at him, her bottom lip trembling.

He stopped opposite her. Their faces were centimetres apart. She could smell coffee on his breath, and a faint waft of body odour. She knew there was a good chance he would try to kiss her, if he could. But she wasn't going to let him do that.

All of a sudden, Angel looked over his shoulder and fixed her face in an expression of alarm. The guard spun around – and from that moment he didn't stand a chance. Quickly, ruthlessly, Angel grabbed the chain from its hiding place around her waist. She looped it through the bars, around the guard's neck and back into the cell. The guard shouted out and tried to turn, but by now Angel was twisting the two ends of the chain so it tightened against the guard's throat. He tried to grab it and pull it away from his skin but it was too tight, and there was no way Angel was going to loosen it. Not yet.

In the opposite cell, Woody stood up. He watched impassively as the guard gurgled and struggled. Angel could feel her opponent growing weaker. She had no desire to kill the man. Despite everything, he was a police officer, and probably following orders. So as soon as his body went limp and the gurgling stopped, and she knew he had lost consciousness, she released the tension on the chain. She unwound it and put her arms through the bars and under the guard's armpits. She helped him slide to the floor, unconscious. Once he was down, she went through his pockets. It only took a few seconds to locate his bunch of keys. She took them out and, hooking her arm around the bars, tried three different keys before she found the one that opened her door. She dragged the guard into the cell and relieved him of his handgun. She took the chain from around his neck, stepped out of the cell, locked it again, then released Woody. As he stepped out of the cell, Woody looked at his watch. 'Seven minutes, thirty-five seconds. Not bad.'

The guard was stirring. They had to move quickly.

'I'm not going to lie, Woody,' Angel said as she handed him the chain. 'Might be a bit tasty, getting out of this place.'

'Ah, c'mon,' Woody said. 'The BOPE might have automatic weapons, but you've got a handgun and I'm armed with an old toilet chain. What could possibly go wrong?'

Angel didn't reply. Instead she raised her weapon and moved quickly along the corridor, away from the cells.

14

Impact

The cadets kept to the shadows.

They moved with the stealth of a military unit. Lukas and Sami took the lead. They advanced with their assault rifles engaged, panning the area ahead. Abby, Lili and Tommy followed. Abby guided Tommy, one hand on his forearm. Lili held her weapon loosely across her chest. Max took up the rear. Every ten paces he stopped, his weapon raised, and looked behind him for threats.

The roads were completely deserted. People must be sheltering from the firefight, Max thought. The buildings were shocking, the smell of waste intense. They moved unnoticed to the end of a shabby, empty alleyway and stopped where the alley met a wider street.

'I think we need to follow that road then hang a right,' Tommy said.

Lukas scowled as he looked around the corner and examined the road. 'It's too busy,' he said. 'If we walk down there carrying automatic weapons, we'll stick out a mile.'

'He's right,' Abby said. 'We'll have to ditch the weapons.'

'But we might need them,' Lili said. 'Why don't we disassemble them and stow them in our rucksacks?'

It was a good idea. The cadets took cover behind a pile of bin bags. Abby kept watch while the others crouched down, removed the magazines from their weapons, took their rifles apart and packed them in their rucksacks.

Max was getting to his feet when he heard shouting. He recognised the shrill voice. 'Guzman!' There was the unmistakable sound of Guzman's Uzi as the gang leader fired two short bursts. Shouts of alarm filled the air, and people ran down the road where the cadets were hiding behind the bin bags. Above it all they could hear Guzman's insane shouting – and it was getting closer.

'We need to hide,' Max said.

'Where?' Lukas said.

Sami pointed across the road towards a side street that was overgrown with dense vegetation. 'There,' he said.

Lukas frowned. 'Are you joking? Have you seen how many sewage pipes run into it?'

'He's right,' Lili said. 'The best place to hide is somewhere nobody wants to go. Quick – we need to run!'

As if to highlight the urgency, there was another burst of Uzi fire – much closer this time. The cadets hauled their rucksacks over their shoulders and sprinted. The road was chaos. Kids were running away from the sound of the gunfire, but that worked to the cadets' advantage, because they were just five more people in a panicking crowd and they went unnoticed. Lili led them at a breathless pace, at right angles to the flow of the crowd. As they approached the side street, the stench became almost unbearable. But she was right. The stinking vegetation was their best chance of staying hidden.

The cadets plunged into the greenery. It grew up to Max's waist and was marshy underfoot. As they disturbed the undergrowth, swarms of insects flew up around them. They buzzed and whined in Max's face and eyes, and he felt them biting. He could also hear Guzman's voice, almost as high-pitched as the insects.

Lili shouted, 'Dive!'

He dived.

The foliage was soft and wet. Max landed on his front, facing away from the street. Abby was next to him. They wriggled around in an attempt to see back out. The movement released a putrid stench from underneath them. Max gagged and tried not to think about the filth in which he was lying.

'Hey, Max,' Abby whispered. 'As first dates go, I'd say this was a bit of a stinker.'

'Abby, there's something I need to say . . .'

'I know, I know,' Abby replied. 'I know we can never be a thing. Hector would never allow it.'

'We've got to do the right thing, Abby. We've got to think about the group, not just us.'

'I get it,' Abby said. She hesitated. 'I enjoyed that kiss though.'

Max was about to say, 'Me too.' But he didn't, because suddenly Guzman was there.

He was standing at the entrance to the side road. Max could just see him through the thick vegetation. The moonlight reflected in his wild eyes and glinted off his chunky gold necklace. He held his Uzi loosely by his side as he peered down the side street, scanning the foliage. Behind him were five or six Blue Command gang members. They were glancing at each other, perhaps worried that Guzman would send them into the foul-smelling foliage to search for the cadets. Max thought about getting his weapon from his rucksack and reassembling it. He didn't want to hit any of the gang members or even Guzman. But maybe, if it came to it, he could lay down some suppressive fire . . .

'Nothing to see here,' Abby whispered. 'Just me and Max having a nice little chat. Move along now . . .'

Guzman raised his weapon. Max froze. He realised Guzman was about to spray a burst in their direction. 'Get down!' he whispered, and pressed himself into the ground, his face making contact with the foetid mud. The sound of the Uzi rang out: the harsh coughing of three separate bursts. Max fully expected to be hit. But then there was movement next to him. Abby squirmed in close and wrapped her arms around his head, to protect it.

He heard, rather than saw, ricocheting off the walls on either side. Then he felt Abby judder. She hissed in pain. With a cold, sinking feeling in the pit of his stomach, Max realised she'd been hit, probably by a ricochet. It took every ounce of his willpower not to move. Guzman was shouting again, but his voice was receding. When, thirty seconds later,

Max dared to look, Guzman was no longer there. Nor were his guys. They'd moved on.

He turned to Abby, who was shivering badly, her face white with shock. She was holding her right upper arm and blood was seeping through her fingertips. She gave Max a weak smile. 'Better my arm,' she said in a small, shaky voice, 'than your head.'

Max swore. There was a bloodied bullet on the ground. He knelt next to Abby. He rifled through his rucksack and grabbed his med pack, then opened it and pulled out a bandage. Gently, he moved Abby's hand and tore into her long-sleeved cream top to reveal the wound. It was bleeding profusely, but the blood flowed slowly and was a deep, sludgy colour, not a bright, fast-flowing red. 'It's not an arterial bleed,' he said. 'I think the bullet just grazed you. The ricochet must have slowed its speed. We were lucky.'

His fingers were covered in her blood, which smeared over her clothes as he helped her slide her wounded arm out of the sleeve. She winced, but didn't cry out – even when Max put pressure on the wound to stop it bleeding. The others were standing around them now, their faces creased with anxiety.

'Is . . . is she going to be okay?' Tommy said.

'Ah, sure,' Abby managed to whisper. 'What's a bullet wound between friends?'

Nobody laughed. Max grabbed the bandage and wrapped it tightly around the wound. Abby's eyes bulged with pain, but she didn't complain. All she said was, 'We need to get to that warehouse.'

'Forget it,' Max said. He looked up at Tommy. 'I'm sorry, mate,' he said. 'Abby needs proper medical care. We need to get her out of the favela.'

'Sure. I underst—'

Abby pushed herself up with her good arm. 'What the hell are you talking about, Max?' she said. Her usual fire had returned, for now at least.

'You're hurt,' Max said. 'We need to –'

'You think, just because I kissed you, you have to act the knight in shining armour?'

'Abby, you've been shot.'

'You said it yourself – it's just a graze.'

'I only said that because . . .' Max stopped and looked at the others. 'Back me up here, guys,' he said.

'Can you walk?' Lili asked. She held out an arm and helped Abby to her feet.

'I feel like I've been lying in a toilet. Disgusting,' Abby said. She looked very shaky as she turned to Max. 'Seriously,' she said, 'I'm fine. Let's get going.'

'This is insane,' Max muttered. But he knew there was no point arguing with her, and it looked as if the others were on her side. He nodded curtly and looked back down the side street. Abby gave him a thin smile. He could tell she was in more pain than she was letting on. But her expression was determined.

'Okay. Let's go,' he said.

15

Pepe's Penalty

Angel and Woody moved quickly, in absolute silence. There was a door at the end of the corridor where the holding cells were located. It was unguarded – at least, it was now they'd overcome the guard. Angel held the weapons he'd confiscated in both hands, scanning the area ahead as they advanced. Woody held the toilet chain loosely in his right hand, ready to use it if he needed to.

They reached a staircase and moved stealthily up it. On the ground floor they came to a set of double doors. There was a small glass panel in each one, through which they could see two BOPE officers. Woody and Angel stood on either side of the doors, their backs to the wall. Woody tapped gently on the door. One of the BOPE officers turned, opened it and stepped through. He looked at Angel in surprise.

She winked at him.

The guard never knew what hit him.

Angel pivoted on her left foot, raised her right leg and

kicked the guard hard in the stomach. He doubled over in pain and she cracked the butt of her pistol down on the back of his skull. He was lying in a heap on the floor by the time the second guard knew that anything was wrong. He burst through the double doors at the same time that Woody whipped the toilet chain. It curled around the guard's neck. Woody tugged the guard towards him and elbowed him in the face. The guard's eyes rolled, and he collapsed to the floor next to his mate.

By now Angel was through, her weapon engaged. They were in the main entrance to the building. There was nobody in here – the two guards they had put down had obviously been the only security here – but they could see the shadows of more personnel through the frosted-glass entrance doors fifteen metres from their position. Angel counted four guys. They showed no sign that they knew Angel and Woody were escaping.

Angel looked up. There were two panel lights in the ceiling – the only light sources in the room. She pointed her weapon at one light, then nodded at Woody. He moved to the main entrance and stood to its right. 'Go!' he whispered.

Angel discharged a round from her handgun into each of the panel lights. There was a brief shower of sparks from each light, then the room went dark. The shadows on the other side of the frosted glass turned. One of the guards shouted. The door opened and two of them ran in. Bad move. With the aid of the toilet chain, Woody had them on the ground, unconscious, in under five seconds. If the remaining two had been smarter, they would have moved away. But they weren't, and they didn't. They presented themselves at the main entrance side by side. Angel put one of the guards down with an elbow in the face. Woody worked his magic with the toilet chain on the other.

Now there were four unconscious guards on the floor and no sign of any more. Angel could hear traffic. She covered the exit with her handgun while Woody stole a further pistol and two MP5 submachine guns from the guards he'd just put down. He handed one of the MP5s to Angel, and they prepared to burst out of the building.

Their mistake was not looking back. With all their focus on escaping the BOPE's headquarters, they didn't realise that one of the guards had regained consciousness. He shouted at them, and out of the corner of her eye Angel saw he was pointing his weapon at them.

If they hadn't thrown themselves through the doorway, Angel would have been dead. The guard's bullet landed where her head had just been. But she and Woody hurled themselves forward just in time. They rolled down the stone steps in front of the building. Angel's cheek slammed against one of the steps, sending a shriek of pain through her head and down her spine. The world spun. By the time it was still again, she and Woody were at the base of the steps, looking up. The guard was there. His weapon was engaged. He was pointing it at them.

There was no time for either of them to raise their own weapons. They were disorientated and at a disadvantage.

A fatal disadvantage.

Angel felt ice in her stomach. She knew the end was about to come.

* * *

Pepe watched it all happen, open-mouthed.

He had crossed the busy road and was now standing opposite the entrance to the BOPE's headquarters, next to a black SUV whose engine was still warm. He was bouncing his football, but really he was only half aware of it. He was transfixed by the sight of the two British people who had tumbled down the stone steps, and by the BOPE guard standing over them, his weapon raised.

Pepe had lived in the favela long enough to know how this story would end.

It was all his fault. If he hadn't gone to the gang members, none of this would have happened. Hadn't they warned him often enough? Hadn't his mum and dad warned him for as long as he could remember?

You end up paying the penalty.

The BOPE guy moved his weapon from the woman to the man, then back to the woman again.

Pepe blinked, then looked at the football in his hands.

The penalty.

Suddenly he knew what he had to do.

It was instinctive. He had done it often enough in the streets of the favela after all.

He dropped the football, let it bounce once, then kicked it.

For a moment, Pepe thought he had put too much curve on the ball. But he hadn't. It curled towards the BOPE guy. Pepe heard the leathery thud as it slammed into the side of his face. He was just in time. The ball knocked the police officer sideways as he fired his weapon. The bullet missed

141

the woman by a hand's breadth. Pepe saw it spark on the ground then ricochet away. He allowed himself a smile, but the smile soon faded when he saw the police officer, startled and angry, turn and point his weapon at Pepe.

And that was his big mistake.

The British couple pushed themselves up and flew at the BOPE officer, tackling him to the ground. He fired again. This time he hit the windscreen of the SUV next to Pepe. It shattered, but by now the BOPE officer was on his back. The man kicked him in the ribs while the woman removed his weapon.

More BOPE officers arrived. Three, four, five, spewing from the building, shouting. Pepe watched in horror as the man and the woman raised their weapons towards them.

Were they really going to shoot all those police officers? Didn't they know what would happen to them if they did?

They fired towards the police building. The bullets fell above the BOPE, and on the steps in front of them. None of them hit the police officers, but the attack was enough to force them all to the ground, crouching in defensive positions. The man and woman stepped backwards as they fired. In a few seconds, they were alongside Pepe.

His football rolled back to him. He picked it up, then the woman grabbed him. The man continued to fire warning shots at the BOPE. Pepe and the woman were almost at the main road. The woman stepped out onto it, weapon engaged. A white Range Rover screeched to a halt. She pulled open the driver's door and ripped the driver from his position behind the wheel. He staggered to the pavement as other cars beeped or swerved around the Range Rover. The British man was still firing as the woman bundled Pepe into the back of the car then shouted an instruction at her partner. He lowered his weapon and, as the woman took the wheel, ran across the road and dived into the passenger seat.

The Range Rover's wheels spun with a high-pitched squeal as the vehicle accelerated. Timidly, Pepe peered through the side window. The BOPE were getting back to their feet.

Then they were out of sight, and the Range Rover was speeding down the road. For a blissful moment, Pepe thought the English couple were driving him to safety. But the woman swung the vehicle sharply to the left, off the main road and back towards the favela.

A mobile phone was in a magnetic holder on the dashboard. It was unlocked. The man grabbed it and dialled a number.

'Hector?' he roared into the handset. 'It's Woody. We've got a problem. Get the chopper ready. We're going in!'

16

Snakes and Ladders

The hardest part of staying incognito was hiding Abby's wound. It was obviously worse than she was letting on. Anybody who looked closely at her would see she was struggling. Her face was pale and sweating, her gait uncertain, as though she was dizzy. Occasionally her eyes rolled.

Nobody *did* look closely, however. Guzman's gunfire seemed to have scared the young people in the streets, even though they almost all wore Blue Command bandanas. Children scurried into doorways and down alleys. Older youths ran in all directions. Only the beggars stayed where they were.

So the cadets, still shouldering their heavy rucksacks, and Tommy were able to move unnoticed. Even so, they kept to the shadows as they turned into the main street and headed along it. They passed buildings so dilapidated that Max found himself wondering if they really housed humans.

The stench of sewage was all-pervading now, although he realised that he could be smelling himself and the other cadets. They were truly filthy.

They turned right. This was the road Tommy had said they needed to follow to find his girlfriend. At the end was the largest building they had seen in the favela. It looked like a flat-roofed barn, with walls made of huge sheets of corrugated iron. The cadets were looking at it end-on, so they couldn't see how long it was. Vast double doors faced them, and five armed Blue Command personnel guarded it. Even from a distance, Max could tell they were on high alert. They were like wolves prowling around their territory, panning the area with their weapons. Were they expecting an attack? Or had they heard that Guzman was on the rampage, and were worried about what would happen if they weren't seen to be doing their job properly?

Distant gunfire. The cadets pressed themselves against a wall while the Blue Command guys pointed their weapons down the street.

'Is this the place?' Lukas said quietly.

'I think it must be,' Lili said. 'Look.' She pointed up at the flat roof of the building. Silhouetted against the night sky, huge bundles of cables threaded in through the roof from all directions. They looked almost snake-like. There was also, just visible, the upper curve of a satellite dish.

'That's communications gear,' Sami said. 'Tommy's right. This must be where Blue Command broadcast their pirated TV channels from.'

'We have to get in there,' Tommy announced, too loudly

for Max's liking. He started to step forward, out of the shadows, before Lukas grabbed him and pushed him roughly against the wall.

'Stay where you are,' Lukas said, 'unless you want those guys to shoot you in the head.'

Abby was shaking. Max put an arm around her. 'We have to get you out of here,' he whispered.

'This job needs all of us,' Abby said wearily. 'Look how heavily guarded it is. And we can't leave Tommy's girlfriend to these people. Think what will happen to her. Don't argue with me, Max.'

Max knew she was right. He nodded. 'I think we need to get onto the roof,' he said.

'Right,' Lili agreed. 'There must be an access point where those cables enter the building.'

'And some way to get up there to fix the cables.'

'We can't approach from this direction,' Sami said. 'The guards will see us. We need to get around to the side or the back.'

Nobody disagreed. They retreated stealthily, Max holding Abby steady and Lukas keeping a stern eye on Tommy in case he tried anything stupid. They cut around several bullet-marked, graffiti-strewn buildings, using their internal compasses to skirt around the communications warehouse, keeping to the darkest, most desolate side streets.

It was five minutes before the warehouse came into view again, at the end of a stinking alleyway. The cadets fought their way along it, holding their breath. They emerged by the warehouse. To their right they could make out the Blue

146

Command guards at the front. They were facing away from the cadets, who were able to creep around the warehouse unseen.

At the back they encountered five kids, probably no older than ten years old. The kids scurried away into the maze of the favela the moment they saw the cadets approach. No doubt they mistook them for older Blue Command personnel, which suited the cadets fine, because here, at the back of the building, was a metal access ladder, precariously fixed to the roof and leading all the way down to the ground.

Wordlessly, the cadets made a collective decision to climb it. Lili went first. The ladder wobbled as she ascended, but she was fast and lithe and was on the roof within thirty seconds. Abby went next, Max close behind her, ready to catch her if she fell. Climbing one-handed, she nearly did, but Max was there, supporting her to stay on the wobbly rungs. It was with relief that they tumbled onto the roof.

Lili had already reassembled the rifle from her rucksack and was examining the two sturdy bolts that fastened the ladder to the roof. It would take a heavy spanner to loosen them. Abby crouched, breathing heavily. Max clicked his assault rifle together as Tommy, then Lukas, then Sami, joined them on the roof.

'Cover the back,' Max told Lukas. Lukas nodded, assembled his weapon and got down on one knee, his rifle engaged and pointing towards the ladder. Lili put her arm around Abby, checking she was okay. Max, Sami and Tommy advanced along the roof, bending low. The communications satellite was set back from the front edge and the mass of cabling entered the building next to it. There were five bundles of black cables, each as thick as a drainpipe. They emitted an electric hum. A circular rubber housing protected the entry point from the elements. Just behind it was a metal panel set into the roof – a roof hatch! Two iron bars opposite each other acted as a handle to lift it.

Max grabbed the bars. Sami pointed his weapon at the panel.

Max opened the panel a crack. Light flooded out from the warehouse. Max peered in. The interior was vast, well-lit and at least fifteen metres high. In the middle, in a line across the warehouse, were three long trestle tables. One was covered with tools: wrenches and screwdrivers, hammers and soldering irons. Another bowed under the weight of rolls of thick black cable. On the third table were several laptops and TV monitors. Max couldn't see what the monitors showed, but they emitted a flickering glow.

Between the trestle tables and the back of the warehouse, the bundles of cables descended from the ceiling to a collection of vast junction boxes, each one the size of a small car. The room was illuminated by four bright lamps, one in each corner. A power cable snaked from each lamp into the centre, meeting out of sight under the middle trestle table. Between the tables and the front entrance were two video cameras on tripods.

And alone in the warehouse was a girl.

She had raven-black hair down to the middle of her back, and she was leaning over one of the trestle tables with a soldering iron. Max couldn't see what she was working on.

He could see, however, that they had a big problem.

A square metal frame was fixed to the ceiling, surrounding the roof hatch. A thick chain was attached to a carabiner on the frame. The chain extended down to the girl, where it was fastened to an iron band locked around her waist. She was able to move around the warehouse, but how far was limited by the length of the chain. She could access the tools around her. She could work. But she couldn't leave.

Max turned to Tommy. 'Is that her?' he whispered.

Tommy joined him at the open hatch and looked down. 'Beatriz,' he whispered. He looked at Max, clearly shocked by what he saw. Then, much louder, he called, '*Beatriz!*'

'*Quiet!*' Max hissed. But it was too late. The girl looked around, obviously expecting to see somebody inside the warehouse. Only when it became apparent that there was nobody did she look up to the ceiling. Max saw her face for the first time. She was unexpectedly pale. Her skin was smudged with dirt and her hair looked matted. Her tired eyes widened as she saw the two faces looking down at her from the ceiling.

'*Tommy?*' she mouthed. She looked sharply towards the main entrance of the warehouse, then back up at the ceiling. She made a shooing gesture with her hands. 'Go!' she mouthed. 'They have guns!'

Max lowered the panel and turned to Tommy. 'She speaks good English?'

'Fluent,' Tommy said. 'I told you, she's a brainbox. How will we get her out of there?'

Max thought hard. Beatriz wasn't going anywhere until

they could disconnect her from that chain. There were, to his mind, only two ways to do that. Either they cut the chain where it was attached to Beatriz or they unclipped the carabiner where it met the frame on the ceiling. But the frame was well out of their reach. Max couldn't think of a way to get to it.

Tommy stared at him, looking frightened. 'She's stuck there, isn't she?' he said.

'Unless we can cut that chain, yes.'

'Then what are we going to do? I'm not leaving without her.'

Max looked around, across the rooftops of the favela. It crossed his mind that if they could remove the ladder from the wall of the warehouse, they could use it to cross the gap to the next building, then escape across the rooftops, safely away from the dangers of the street.

But at the moment, they could only do that without Beatriz.

'What are we going to do?' Tommy repeated, deep worry lines etched on his brow. 'Maybe I can call down to the guards at the front and talk them round . . .'

'Are you crazy?' Max said. 'Don't move.' He looked back at the panel. He felt strangely calm. There was no sign of Guzman. There was no indication that the BOPE were nearby. Maybe, just maybe, they had enough time to sneak Beatriz out from under the BOPE's noses.

'I'm going down there,' he said.

17

A Leap of Faith

The cadets assembled in the middle of the roof. Max explained to them what he and Tommy had seen. 'So this is the plan,' he said.

'There's a plan?' Abby said with a wan smile. 'I thought we were making this up as we went along.' She was sweating badly. Her lips were pale. It pained Max to see her in this state, trying to pretend that nothing was wrong. He forced himself to concentrate. The sooner they could rescue Beatriz, the sooner they could be out of this cursed favela.

'I'm going to open the panel in the roof,' he continued, 'and call down to Beatriz to throw up one of the big loops of cable that are down there. Lukas, you're the strongest. If I hold one end of the cable, you can lower me down, right?'

Lukas nodded.

'Once I'm down there, I'll try to find some way of cutting through the chain that's holding Beatriz. I'll also look for a spanner that we can use to loosen that ladder. I think it's too short for us to put it through the roof and use it to escape the warehouse, but it'll stop anyone else getting up here, and we might be able to use it to get across the rooftops if we need to. Once I've freed Beatriz, Lukas can pull us back up through the roof and we'll get the hell out of here.'

'We'll have to be quiet,' Lili said. 'If the guards hear us, they'll shoot.'

Max nodded. 'I'll have my weapon,' he said quietly.

'What if the guards walk in while you're in there?'

'It's a risk,' Max admitted. 'But I don't think it's likely. They've got Beatriz on a leash so they won't be expecting her to escape. And I don't think they know we're up here. If they expect an attack from anywhere, it'll be from the front.'

'We should still be on our guard,' Lili said. 'Sami, you cover the back. I'll cover the front. We can lay down suppressive fire if we need to.'

'What can I do?' Tommy asked. 'I want to help.'

There was a brief pause. The cadets looked at each other. The best thing Tommy could do would be to stay well out of the way while they got to work, but nobody wanted to say that. It was Abby who finally spoke. 'Your job is to look after me,' she said. 'I'm not going to lie – I feel a bit under the weather.' She looked down at her wounded arm. Blood had started to seep through the bandage. Tommy swallowed hard, then nodded.

'Okay,' Max said. 'Let's do it.'

The cadets moved in absolute silence: Sami to the back

of the roof, Lili to the front, Lukas and Max to the metal panel. Max lifted it away fully this time. Beatriz was below, looking up at them with an expression of pure alarm, then at the main doors, then back up again. Max pointed at the table that held the rolls of cable and gave what he hoped was an encouraging nod.

She frowned.

'Throw it up!' Max mouthed, gesturing with his hands.

Beatriz tilted her head, as if she didn't understand what he was saying. She obviously did though, because she hurried over, lifted a roll of cable and gave Max an inquisitive look. Max nodded and gave her a thumbs-up. Beatriz glanced nervously at the door again. She swung the roll of cable under her legs to give it some momentum and then hurled it up towards the opening in the roof.

It missed. Badly. The roll crashed against the roof of the warehouse and fell back to the ground, where it clattered into another trestle table. Max winced at the noise, held his breath and half shut the panel in case anybody came to investigate. Nobody did. He opened the panel and Beatriz tried again.

This time her aim was good. The roll soared up to the opening in the roof and Max grabbed it with one hand. 'Hope it's long enough,' he said as he handed it to Lukas.

The roll was held together with a plastic cable tie, which Lukas cut with the knife from his pack while Max disassembled his rifle again and stowed it in his rucksack. Together they unfurled the cable. Max took the leading end and wrapped it around his waist and across his chest and back. The cable was too stiff to tie into a knot, so he gripped the end firmly with his right hand and nodded at Lukas. 'Ready?'

'Ready.'

'Here goes nothing. Don't drop me, hey?'

'I'll do my best,' Lukas said without smiling. He gripped the cable. 'Go.'

Gingerly, Max lowered himself through the opening, holding on to the roof with his left hand. It took a great leap of faith to let go of the edge, but he took a deep breath and did it. Immediately he was swinging in mid-air like a pendulum.

He was grateful to Lukas for letting him down quickly and smoothly. He didn't relish the thought of being suspended in the middle of that warehouse, an easy target, for a second longer than necessary. As soon as his feet touched the ground, he unwound the cable from his body and left it hanging in the air. He turned to Beatriz, who was staring at him, wide-eyed. 'Who are you?' she whispered.

'I'm a friend of Tommy's.'

'That tells me nothing. Who *are* you?'

'Nobody,' Max said. He took off his rucksack, removed the assault rifle from inside and reassembled it. Then he approached the trestle table that was covered with tools. He grabbed a sturdy adjustable spanner and looked up at the hole in the ceiling. Lukas was there, looking down. Max showed him the spanner, then hurled it up to him. Lukas caught it, then disappeared.

'Let's get you out of here,' Max said. He walked up to

Beatriz and examined the chain that attached her to the roof. 'We need to cut through this,' he said.

Beatriz stared at him and blinked. 'That's your big plan?' she whispered. She barely had an accent. 'You think I have not tried to do that already? Look!' She showed him various points in the chain where it was dented and marked. Then she waved one arm to indicate the warehouse in general. 'There isn't a tool in here I haven't tried!'

Max blushed. For some reason it hadn't occurred to him that Beatriz would have attempted this herself. But he didn't have time to say anything, because at that precise moment, the door opened.

A single Blue Command guard appeared. He didn't seem to be expecting anything untoward because he was not holding a weapon and was walking with a relaxed, almost arrogant gait. He wore a bandana, of course, but no top. His right arm was covered with tattoos. He froze when he saw Max looking at him, then snarled. Max raised his weapon quickly and pointed it at the guard. 'Tell him to get out,' he said to Beatriz.

Beatriz translated. The guard turned quickly and scurried out of the warehouse. From the roof, Max had not been able to see the doors. Now he saw that they opened inwards and there was a long, solid beam of wood on a hinge to one side that acted as a primitive lock. At the moment it pointed upwards, but if he swung it down he could lock them into the warehouse.

His weapon pointing ahead, he ran to the door. Voices shouted urgently outside. Somebody shouted, 'Guzman!'

Max fired a warning round into the wall above the door. The retort echoed around the warehouse. He reached the door and slammed it shut, then swung the wooden bolt down, barring the door. Just in time. Gunshots sounded from outside.

Max ran back to Beatriz. Her face was panicked. He looked up at the hole in the ceiling. Lukas was there.

'What's happening?' his friend asked.

'We're blown!' Max shouted. 'Pull the ladder up before they get up there!'

Sami had the spanner and was straining to loosen the first bolt when he heard gunfire. It sounded like it was coming from inside the warehouse.

'Max,' he whispered.

He turned. He wanted to run back to the hole in the roof and do whatever was necessary to help and protect his mate. But Lukas shouted at him. 'Get the ladder up! *Get it up! Now!*'

Max spun. He took in the contents of the warehouse again. The communications cables snaking down from the ceiling. The video cameras. The lights. The trestle tables full of tools. Beatriz. She was breathing heavily, her eyes darting around. She looked terrified, but also determined.

There was a banging on the door. More gunfire.

'You've got to get out of here,' Beatriz said. She pointed helplessly at the chain attaching her to the roof. 'I'm stuck here, but they can pull you back up through the roof.'

Was she right? Was that really their only option?

Max didn't think so. He pointed at the communications cables. 'Those things distribute pirated TV around the favelas, right?'

'Yeah.'

Max moved over to the video cameras. 'Can you connect the cables to these cameras?'

Beatriz nodded mutely.

Max closed his eyes and breathed deeply as he tried to think. A series of images flashed across his mind. He saw Pepe at the safe house, staring at the blank TV, uselessly pointing the remote control at it. He saw Guzman – crazy eyes and wild hair. He saw the Jackal with the silver insignia on his BOPE balaclava.

And all of a sudden, a way out of this impossible situation suggested itself. He strode over to the centre of the warehouse and looked up at the hole in the ceiling. Lukas was there, still clutching the cable Max had used to descend. He looked panicky and was mouthing the words, 'Get back up!'

Max shook his head. 'I need Guzman,' he called up. 'I need the Jackal. And I need time.'

For a moment, Max thought Lukas was going to argue. But he didn't. He simply nodded, and disappeared.

Desperately, Sami continued to unscrew the first bolt. It came off easily, but the second was a more difficult proposition. It wouldn't budge. He twisted as hard as he could, but to no avail.

Voices, shouting, down below. Sami didn't even have time

157

to look over the edge. He knew the Blue Command kids were coming. Any moment now, they'd be up the ladder and on the roof. If that happened, it would be game over.

He stood up and kicked the end of the spanner. It budged a fraction. He held his breath then kicked again. More movement. On his knees, he twisted the final bolt by hand as fast as he could. By now, Lili was beside him. She grabbed one side of the ladder as Sami grabbed the other. As they hauled it up, Sami peeked over the edge. He saw three armed gang members down there. One of them was jumping to try and grab the ladder, but it was just out of reach. Sami leaned back as one of the others raised his weapon and fired into the air. 'What's happening with Max?' Sami demanded as he and Lili pulled the ladder up.

'He's still inside,' Lili said. 'He's refusing to come up.'

'What do you mean?' Sami said. Stepping backwards, they dragged the heavy ladder onto the roof. There was another burst of fire from down below.

'He won't leave Beatriz. He's given Lukas some instructions. I don't know what yet.' She looked him straight in the eye. 'I think he's got a plan,' she said.

18

Murder Hole

Abby's body felt ice-cold. The bullet wound in her arm was throbbing. She was dizzy. At any other time, she would have been irritated by somebody like Tommy putting his arm around her shoulders and quietly and calmly telling her to breathe deeply. Right now he was a comfort.

She was only vaguely aware of what was happening on the roof. The ladder was lying next to her. Sami was somewhere behind. Lukas and Lili were in front of her, each at one corner of the building. They held their weapons high and pointing downwards, as though preparing to fire at whoever was on the ground.

A wave of nausea passed over her. She drew a deep breath and looked up. She could see the stars, bright and numerous. They were beautiful. Much more beautiful than this stinking favela. Had they really only spent a night here? It felt like much longer than that. Days. Weeks. She was so tired. Perhaps she should just lie down here, look at the stars and fall asleep.

'Wake up!' Tommy said, and he shook her. There was gunfire. That, more than Tommy's encouragement, forced Abby to rouse herself. She looked around sharply. Everything was spinning.

'Are you okay?' Tommy said 'Abby, are you okay?'

She nodded woozily. She could hear someone shouting. It was Lili.

'What's she saying?' Abby mumbled.

Lukas was at the front left corner of the building, Lili at the front right.

There was a low wall around the perimeter of the roof, about a foot high. There were square holes in it, no bigger than a hardback book. They were just large enough for the barrel of an assault rifle to poke through and for the user to see the street below through the weapon's sights.

'Murder holes,' Sami had said moments before. 'Holes in buildings to point guns through. In Syria, they were everywhere.'

Lukas and Lili lay on their fronts, their weapons pointing through the murder holes.

There were about fifteen Blue Command gang members at the front of the warehouse now. They were keeping their distance from the main entrance, and shouting at each other. As Lukas watched, he saw three of them approach the door.

Lukas wasn't certain how many rounds he had left. He would have to use them sparingly. He switched his weapon to the semi-automatic setting and released a single warning shot onto the ground between the gang members and the front entrance. The three gang members scampered back. The others melted into the shadow of a building opposite. A couple of them raised their own weapons, but there was nothing to shoot at: Lukas and Lili were invisible, protected by the wall around the perimeter of the roof.

If Max wants time, Lukas thought, he gets time.

But that wasn't all he wanted.

'Lili,' Lukas called, 'you need to call down to them in Portuguese.'

'And say what?'

'Say that we need Guzman and the Jackal. Say that if they come, we'll give ourselves up.'

Lili hesitated. 'Are you sure that's a good idea?'

'Since you ask,' Lukas said, 'I think it's a terrible idea. But our only other choice is to get off this rooftop and leave Max to his fate.' He looked back over his shoulder at Abby. 'And Max isn't the only one who might not make it,' he muttered before shouting across at Lili. 'Can you do it?'

Lili didn't reply immediately, then she shouted something at the Blue Command guys down below. Lukas could only make out the words 'Guzman' and 'BOPE'. He watched the gang members carefully through the sights of his weapon. At first they looked surprised. Then a couple of them grinned. It looked to Lukas as though they thought Lili's request was the height of stupidity. One of them gave an instruction, and four gang members scurried off into the darkness.

'What now?' Lili called.

'Now we wait,' Lukas said. 'And we hope Max knows what he's doing.' He looked over his shoulder again.

'Whatever it is, buddy,' he muttered to himself, 'do it fast. Abby can't last much longer.'

Beatriz was incredible to watch. Despite being limited by the chain attached to the ceiling, she moved around the warehouse quickly and efficiently. Occasionally she would give Max an instruction: 'Move that camera over here.' 'Pass me the soldering iron.' Otherwise, she worked in speedy silence, rewiring cables and soldering components, a pencil behind her ear and a screwdriver between her teeth.

When he wasn't needed, Max kept his rifle trained on the entrance to the warehouse. He trusted the other cadets to keep Blue Command away from the door. When he heard a bark of gunfire from above, he knew they would be doing exactly that. But he had seen the BOPE at work. He knew that when they arrived, they might have armoured vehicles and bulletproof riot shields. They would gain access to this warehouse in an instant, even though it was locked from the inside. The cadets on the roof, and Max with his solitary firearm, would be in no position to stop them.

'How long's it going to take?' Max said.

'Longer than it needs to, if you keep asking me questions,' Beatriz replied.

'A ballpark would be good. It's not like we have all the time in the world here.'

'Ten minutes,' Beatriz said. She glanced at him in a way that made Max decide it wouldn't be a good idea to ask if she could shave a few minutes off that. He went back to watching the door.

'Hey, Max,' she said as she unscrewed a panel in the side of the video camera. 'How did you know I was here?'

'We were sent to rescue Tommy. He wouldn't leave without you.'

She stopped what she was doing. 'Seriously?'

'Seriously. Beatriz, you need to keep working, otherwise –'

'I'm doing it, I'm doing it.' She continued to unscrew the panel. 'He risked his life for me? A poor girl from the favela? I knew he wasn't like other boys. I'll make it up to him when we get out of here.'

A thunder of gunfire outside.

'Let's hope you get the chance,' Max muttered, and as he spoke he heard a voice from above. It was Sami calling down to him.

Max looked up.

'It's Abby,' Sami called. 'She's in a bad way. She's losing a lot of blood.'

Max glanced at the door, then down at his weapon. He knew that what he was about to try was incredibly risky. At some point in the next few minutes, he would have to tell the other cadets to flee the rooftop. Because there was no point in them all dying.

'Use the ladder to get away from the roof,' he called up. 'Get out of the area then switch your phones on again so the Watchers can locate you. Get to the pick-up point and contact Hector.'

'What about you?'

'I'll meet you there,' Max called. Then he muttered to himself, 'Probably.' He could feel the heat of Sami's stare from above. He looked up and did his best to smile. 'Hey, Sami,' he said.

'Yes?'

'Look after Abby for me.'

'Of course.'

'Tell her . . .'

'What?'

'Nothing. Just look after her.'

Sami nodded, then was gone.

It was very clear to Sami that Lukas didn't like the plan. It smacked of leaving a friend in trouble, and the cadets had been trained not to do that. But Max had been clear and Sami trusted him.

Besides, if Abby was going to get off this roof, it had to be now. Her eyes were rolling and she looked like she was about to lose consciousness.

'Sort out the ladder,' Lukas said. 'We'll hold them back as much as possible.' And to ensure that the Blue Command personnel kept their distance, he attempted to fire a round between them and the warehouse. His weapon clicked uselessly. Lukas swore under his breath. 'I'm out of ammunition,' he said.

'Leave your weapon where it is,' Sami said. 'If they see it pointing at them, it will be enough to hold them back. Come and help me with the ladder.'

Lukas nodded. Carefully he propped the rifle so its barrel still poked through the murder hole. Then, bending low, he and Sami retreated to the centre of the roof. Abby was there, shaking terribly. Tommy had one arm around her.

'We have to leave,' Sami told the English boy.

'What about Beatriz?'

'Max will get her out.'

'How?'

Sami fixed him with a serious stare. 'I don't know,' he said.

'What do you mean, you don't know? We can't just leave without any idea of what's happening. I came here to rescue Beatriz!'

'And that's what we're doing, I promise you. We have to trust Max.'

'Trust him? I don't even *know* him.'

'Yeah,' Lukas cut in. 'And he doesn't even know you, or your girlfriend. So ask yourself what he's doing down there, risking his life.'

Tommy had no answer.

'Trust him now?' Lukas muttered, and Tommy nodded.

The ladder was lying alongside them. Lukas and Sami took an end each. They turned it so it was parallel to the long side of the warehouse. Sami checked that Lili was still at her murder hole, then he and Lukas lifted one end of the ladder and fed it through their hands so that it bridged the gap between the warehouse and the roof of the building next to it. The adjoining building was just a little higher, which meant that the ladder sloped upwards as it rested against the edge of the neighbouring roof. The ground below was deserted – none of the Blue Command

165

personnel at the front of the warehouse dared head this way because of the cadets' rooftop firing points. Sami ran over to the front corner of the roof, where Lili was still in position.

'I'm out of ammunition too,' she said.

'Leave your weapon there,' Sami said. 'We have to get out of here.'

She nodded, glanced nervously over at the hole in the roof, then propped up her weapon and scampered back to the ladder with Sami.

They only had one live weapon now: Sami's. He covered the side street below the ladder while Lukas crossed on all fours. The ladder bowed precariously under his weight, but he reached the opposite roof in a few seconds, then turned quickly and held out a hand to indicate that someone else should cross.

'You go,' Sami urged Tommy.

Tommy nodded, clearly nervous. He moved across the ladder much more slowly than Lukas had. Halfway across, his right foot slipped between the rungs. For a horrific moment, Sami thought Tommy was going to fall. But he regained his balance and crossed, shaken but unharmed, to the other side.

Lili had managed to get Abby to her feet. Abby was deathly pale, but she managed to stagger towards the ladder and, with Lili's help, get down on all fours. Lili put a hand on her shoulder. 'I can't take you across,' she said. 'The ladder won't hold us both. Will you be okay?'

Abby didn't answer. Sami wasn't even sure she'd heard

what Lili said. An expression of grim concentration crossed her face. She winced as she stretched out her wounded hand. The ladder wobbled badly. Sami and Lili exchanged a worried look, but all they could do was trust in Abby's ability.

She moved forward. Then she stopped. Sami couldn't see her face now, but her shoulders were trembling. She was breathing heavily.

And then he heard voices.

He realised he had taken his attention away from the side street down below. Nobody had approached from the front of the warehouse, but at the back end of the street were three children. They weren't armed, nor did they wear Blue Command bandanas. But they were drawing attention to Abby on the ladder . . .

Sami raised his weapon. He didn't want to scare the kids, but he had no option. He fired a single round onto the road safely in front of them. They scampered away, but one of them loitered at the end of the street and Sami had to fire a second round.

Only he couldn't. The weapon clicked uselessly. He too was out of ammo.

Abby was halfway across. The boy below, realising he was safe, flew along the side street towards the front of the warehouse. Lukas stretched his arm out, desperately reaching for Abby, but she had stalled, her head low, her whole body shaking.

'You can do it!' Sami shouted. And then, not knowing quite why, he added, 'Think of Max!'

It did the trick. Abby raised her head and moved forward. The ladder wobbled again, but she was suddenly within Lukas's grasp. He took hold of her good arm and, gently but powerfully, helped her onto the opposite rooftop, where she collapsed in exhaustion.

Lili went next. Cat-like, she was over the ladder in seconds. Sami slung his weapon across his back. He might be out of ammo, but it could still act as a deterrent if somebody saw him with it. Clambering onto the ladder, he started to crawl. But he was only halfway across when, looking left, he saw the kid who had run around to the front. He was standing at the end of the street, pointing up at Sami and shouting to someone out of Sami's sight. Sami crawled fast across the ladder. As he reached the next building, out of the corner of his eye he saw a gunman appear. He hurled himself onto the roof just in time: a hail of bullets flew through the air and hit the ladder, which exploded and fell noisily onto the street below.

Breathlessly, Sami looked at the others, who were crouching low, ready to receive him. 'They know we've left the roof,' he said. 'There's nothing to stop them advancing on Max!'

Abby was clutching her wound. More blood was seeping through her fingertips. 'We have to help him,' she whispered.

Lukas shook his head. 'No,' he said. 'We have to trust him. He told us to get to the pick-up point. That's what we're going to do.'

And painful though it was, Sami had to agree. He looked across the rooftops. There were several buildings very close to each other, their roofs jumpable, if they gave Abby a lot of help. The favela glowed in the night, illuminated by moonlight.

'Turn your phones on, everyone,' he said. 'And let's move.'

19

Exit Wound

Max heard the gunfire outside, and could figure out what it meant. The Blue Command personnel at the front must have seen the cadets escaping the roof. They knew there was no longer any fire support from the top of the warehouse.

And that meant it was only a matter of time before they came for Max and Beatriz.

'How much longer?' he demanded.

'Four minutes.' Beatriz was sweating heavily and her skin was smeared with dirt. 'What's happening out there?'

There was shouting outside. It was close. Too close.

'I think Blue Command are getting ready to breach the warehouse,' he said.

'You must stop them!' Beatriz said.

'Working on it,' Max muttered. He knelt down and aimed his weapon at the door, just above head height. He fired. A bullet hole appeared. More shouting. Max had the impression that whoever was outside the door was retreating.

He held his position, his finger resting lightly on the trigger of his weapon. 'We don't have four minutes!' he shouted.

'I'm doing my best, okay?' Beatriz's voice was tense. Max could sense her moving about quickly behind him. From the front, another clamour of shouting and the echo of something banging against the front door to the warehouse. Max released another round. The bullet drilled into the front wall just to the left of the first one. Another bullet hole appeared. Again the shouting receded.

But there was a new sound. A mechanical sound. A low, dirty noise. Max couldn't see what vehicle was approaching but he thought he recognised the sound from earlier in the evening, when the BOPE's armoured vehicle had advanced towards the blockade.

'They're here!' he yelled. They only had a few seconds before the BOPE would storm the warehouse. Max decided to release one more round to buy them as much time as possible, but as his finger squeezed the trigger, there was an empty clicking. He was out of ammo.

'Ready!' Beatriz shouted.

Max jumped to his feet and ran back to where Beatriz was standing amid the cables and the cameras, the junction boxes and the TV screens.

He checked everything was in position. Halfway between Beatriz's working area and the entrance to the warehouse, pointing at an angle towards the door, sat a video camera on a tripod, unconnected to anything else. It was set to record, and a red light blinked on the front. Two large TV screens faced the entrance. They were switched off. There were more cameras behind each of the spotlights in the corners of the warehouse. These had cables snaking into Beatriz's complex communications arrangement, but nothing to indicate that they were recording.

Yet.

Max ran to the door and raised the beam of wood that locked the door from the inside. Then he retreated. 'Kill the lights,' he said.

Beatriz flicked a switch to her right. It was only as the bright spotlight in each corner of the room dimmed that Max realised what an electrical hum there had been in the warehouse. The hum faded. Darkness engulfed them, broken only by two beams of light leaking in through the two bullet holes in the front wall. The beams were bright and sharp. There was clearly a strong light source in front of the warehouse. It had to be the armoured vehicle.

'Get ready,' Max whispered. 'This is going to be noisy.' He stood behind Beatriz, put his left arm around her neck and awkwardly held the rifle to her head with his right hand. 'Do exactly what I say.'

He didn't hear Beatriz's reply, because at that moment there was a deafening crash.

The door burst open. The laser beams of light shifted as the end wall of the warehouse buckled and the door crashed open. Max shaded his eyes as the armoured vehicle's lights flooded in through the open door. The vehicle reversed a few metres, then battered the building again. It was more for effect, Max realised, than to create a larger entrance. As it reversed a second time, he saw the silhouettes of

172

several BOPE personnel spill out of their vehicle and rush through the door with bulletproof riot shields. They formed a protective line in front of the entrance while more armed personnel entered and took up firing positions behind them. Max estimated that there were sixteen armed men in total. The headlights flooding through the damaged doorway threw long shadows across the warehouse.

There was a moment of stillness.

Then, from outside, Max heard Guzman's voice.

It was shrill, almost excited. Max saw movement, and the dark outline of Guzman's wild hair at the entrance. 'What's he saying?' he whispered.

'He's shouting at the Jackal,' Beatriz said. And as Guzman continued to shout, she stiffened. 'He's saying: tell your men to open fire.'

Lili led the way over the rooftops of the favela. Sami supported Abby. Lukas stuck with Tommy at the rear. The British boy did not have the cadets' level of fitness, or aptitude and was weak from his imprisonment. It struck Lili that perhaps Lukas was not the best person to be with him. He was the least patient of them all, and he glowered as he urged Tommy on.

They had crossed several rickety rooftops and were at the top of a dilapidated external stone staircase when they heard, from behind, the brutal sound of a collision. They spun around. By the light of the moon, Lili saw that everybody's face bore the same expression of alarm.

'Max?' Abby whispered. Her voice was hoarse and weak.

'We have to keep going,' Lili said. She was hyper-aware of how unconvinced she sounded. Saying they trusted Max was one thing. Leaving him on his own was quite another.

'Come on,' Lukas said. He led Tommy carefully down the staircase into the dark alleyway below. Sami and Abby went next, Sami sweating heavily from the exertion of keeping Abby upright. On the rooftop, Lili heard a second collision and then the unmistakable sound of Guzman's high-pitched voice. She had to stop herself from running back towards the warehouse. She forced herself to descend the steps.

The alleyway was narrow and dark and smelled foul. One end was blocked off by a high breezeblock wall. They moved, as fast as Abby would allow them, to the open end. It led to a slightly wider street. It was not busy, but Lili could see five or six people hurrying through the night, shoulders hunched, heads down, clearly aware that something was going on nearby.

Sami pointed left. 'That way,' he whispered. The cadets nodded and Lili led them into the street.

She had barely gone five paces when it happened. A pedestrian shouted in alarm. Everyone seemed to melt into doorways or side streets. From both ends of the road, figures appeared: police officers in balaclavas, heavily armed. Fifteen of them. Twenty. Maybe more. They all had their weapons aimed at the cadets and they were closing in on them.

Lili twisted around, looking for an escape route. There was none. The houses on either side were dark and closed up. All other pedestrians had disappeared. There were no alleyways or other escape routes. And the BOPE, their weapons engaged, were advancing slowly but inexorably. Their weapons had laser sights. Red dots appeared on the bodies of the cadets, who stood in a ring, facing out, hands in the air.

'Don't fire!' Lili called out in Portuguese. 'We're teenagers. We're unarmed. Please don't fire!'

Nobody replied. The BOPE continued to advance. The little red dots didn't move.

'He's saying, tell your men to open fire – no, wait, the other person is arguing. They can see the camera with the red light. He's saying, they mustn't do anything while we're filming them . . .'

Max licked his lips. If his plan was going to work, he had to move now.

He lowered his weapon. Beatriz staggered back and crouched down under one of the trestle tables. She had wired up a switch there. Max was confident that the BOPE officers wouldn't be able to see it.

He was less confident about what he had to do next.

He remembered, earlier that night, when the Jackal had stared at him across the deserted favela square. How he had raised his hand in a gun shape. The implication had been clear at the time. *I'm going to kill you.*

Max was gambling everything on the Jackal still wanting to do just that.

It was the biggest gamble of his life. No question.

He threw his weapon away. It clattered across the floor

of the warehouse as Max raised his hands. Then he took a couple of paces towards the line of BOPE officers. He could see Guzman just inside the door, and hear him screaming at a taller man to his left.

Max edged towards the blinking camera, just as the taller man behind the BOPE officers came around the defensive line. He had a slow, arrogant gait. As he approached, Max clearly saw the silver insignia on his balaclava.

And the murderous intent in his eyes.

He was carrying a handgun in his right hand. He stopped in front of Max and raised it, so that the barrel was pointing at Max's forehead.

'Do you think I'm stupid, boy?' he said. His English was hesitant and highly accented, but Max was surprised that he spoke any at all.

Max swallowed hard and shook his head.

'Then why do you think I would be stupid enough to fall for a childish trick with a video camera?' He nodded at the camera next to Max.

'I-I didn't,' Max stuttered. 'I –'

'I'm going to enjoy killing you,' the Jackal said.

'No, please . . .'

Before Max could say anything else, the Jackal swung his gun arm to the right and fired into the camera lens. The camera exploded and flew backwards off its tripod.

But Max had already struck.

His unarmed-combat moves, instilled in him since day one in the cadets, were swift, strong and instinctive. With his left arm he grabbed the Jackal's gun wrist. Simultaneously, he lifted his right foot and kicked him sharply in the groin. The Jackal doubled over in pain and Max used his free hand to grab his black balaclava and rip it off his head.

'Now!' he shouted at Beatriz. '*DO IT! NOW!*'

There was the tiny sound of a switch being flicked. The warehouse flooded with light. The two enormous TV screens lit up. They showed the same image, relayed from the other cameras. Guzman, his eyes crazy, waving his submachine gun in the air. The Jackal, his face revealed, turning around, trying to understand what was happening.

And Max, wearing the balaclava so his own face remained anonymous.

Abby's knees buckled. She collapsed to the ground.

Lili shouted again. 'We're unarmed! Don't fire!'

But the only response was the ominous clicking of several weapons being cocked.

'Don't fire! *Don't.*'

Lili hesitated. She could hear . . . *whistling*?

And the regular tapping of a ball bouncing on the ground . . .

She looked past the BOPE officers nearest her. She could see, just beyond them, a kid. He was whistling a jaunty tune and bouncing his football with one hand.

'Pepe?' Lili whispered.

Pepe stopped bouncing the ball. He raised one fist and shouted something in Portuguese. Lili didn't quite catch it, but she suspected it wasn't very polite. The young boy scrambled out of sight, but not before half the BOPE officers had turned to point their weapons at him.

And Lili had recognised his performance for what it was: a distraction.

'Cadets, get ready!' she said quietly.

As she spoke, there was the scream of a vehicle's engine sharply accelerating. A couple of the BOPE guys shouted in alarm as a white SUV reversed fast towards them, scattering BOPE gunmen. It screeched to a halt in front of the cadets. A rear door opened and Woody jumped out. 'Get in!' he shouted.

The cadets ran towards the car. Woody fired his weapon, holding back the BOPE single-handed.

But he wouldn't manage that for long. They had to move.

Sami and Abby were right by Lili, Sami straining to keep Abby on her feet. Lili grabbed her and together they tugged Abby towards the open door, while Woody laid down more rounds, aiming them close enough to the BOPE to keep them scattered, but not so close that he risked hitting any of them. He was screaming at the cadets. '*Get in! Get in the car!*'

And then, somehow, they were inside, huddled together, Abby on Lili's lap and Pepe on Lukas's, Tommy next to them. Angel was in the driving seat, one hand on the wheel, looking back over her shoulder, her face tense with concentration. 'You Tommy?' she said.

Tommy nodded mutely.

'Do exactly what I say. No questions.' She revved the engine heavily and shouted Woody's name above the noise of the gunfire. Then she looked forward suddenly and shouted, '*GET DOWN!*'

The cadets, Pepe and Tommy, cramped in the back seat,

ducked as best they could. A bullet hit the front windscreen. The car shook and a web of cracks spread out from the impact point. A fraction of a second later, Woody was in the passenger seat. It was impossible to see through the glass so he raised his weapon and slammed it against the windscreen, which shattered into a thousand pieces. Angel let out the clutch and the vehicle catapulted forward. There was gunfire from behind as the car screeched to the end of the road and rounded the corner.

'Where's Max?' Angel shouted.

'Long story,' Lili said. 'But we can't go back for him. Abby's lost consciousness. She's losing blood. She needs medical care. *Now!*'

Angel and Woody looked at each other. They nodded. Angel increased their speed.

As they burned down the favela street, the car bumping heavily over the potholes, something caught Lili's eye. Through an open window, for a fraction of a second, she saw a TV. Unlike every other TV she'd seen since arriving in the favela, it was not blank. The screen showed a sharp image of a line of BOPE officers behind riot shields. Of a wild-haired man waving an Uzi in the air. Of a BOPE man, doubled over in pain, bare-faced.

And of a teenager in a Brazilian football top, pulling a black mask with a silver insignia over his head . . .

Then the TV was out of sight, and the tumbledown houses of the favela were whizzing past in a blur.

A grim smile crossed Lili's lips. She finally understood what Max was doing.

'Get us to the pick-up point!' she shouted. 'Max and Beatriz will meet us there.'

'How can you be so sure?' Tommy asked.

'Trust me,' Lili said. 'They'll be there.'

The BOPE guys behind the riot shields blinked in the sudden bright light. Guzman sneered. Close up, Max saw pockmarks on his face and his crooked yellow teeth. The Jackal was a picture of shock and anger. He had distinctive features: a flat nose and heavy eyebrows that met in the middle. A few days' stubble. He raised his weapon so it pointed at Max's chest.

'Before you shoot me,' Max said, as calmly as he could manage, 'you might want to look over there.'

He pointed at the two TV screens. They showed the same image. Max, in a balaclava. Guzman, toting his Uzi. And the Jackal, standing between them, his face on display.

'Smile,' Max said. 'You're on TV. Not just those TVs, by the way. Every TV in the favela, and probably a few more besides.'

The Jackal took a sharp breath. He looked from the TV screens back to Max. 'You're lying,' he said.

Max stared back at him through the eye holes of the balaclava. 'You reckon?'

The Jackal hesitated.

Max tapped the balaclava. 'I know what you're thinking,' he said. 'You're thinking, if only I still had my balaclava on, maybe it wouldn't matter that everyone in the favela who's watching TV now knows that you and your men have the Blue Command leader at gunpoint. You're thinking, if

I don't do the right thing now, my family and I will never be able to show our faces in the favela again. You're thinking, there goes my cushy little arrangement, supporting Guzman and his thugs.'

The Jackal stared at him.

'So what are you going to do, Mr Jackal? Shoot a teenager on live TV? Or do what you should have done ages ago, and arrest Guzman?'

The Jackal didn't have a chance to answer. Guzman had fallen silent. He was looking between the screens and the conversation unfolding between his tame BOPE officer and Max. It wasn't clear whether he understood what Max and the Jackal were saying. But he certainly appeared to have grasped what was going on.

He looked sick.

And when the Jackal lowered his weapon, Guzman lost control.

He raised his Uzi and pointed it, his arm straight, towards Max and the Jackal. The Jackal had his back to him, and Guzman had a direct shot.

He took it.

The burst of 9mm rounds would have ripped into the Jackal's back if Max hadn't moved so fast. He hurled himself at the armed police officer, colliding heavily with him and knocking him off his feet. The bullets drilled harmlessly into the far wall of the warehouse. At the same time, the line of riot shields parted in the middle. The BOPE officer behind the gap had his weapon raised and primed, and he didn't hesitate.

181

A single shot hammered into Guzman's back, between his shoulder blades.

There was a sudden, shocked silence in the warehouse.

Guzman dropped his Uzi. He looked down. Blood bloomed on his shirt. The exit wound was catastrophic. Guzman looked up again, then collapsed to his knees. His hands covered his chest and blood seeped between his fingers. He tried to say something, but all that came from his mouth was a feeble gurgle, then bloodstained foamy spittle. He fell forward. By the time his head hit the ground, he was dead.

There was silence.

Max stood, and so did the Jackal. If he felt any gratitude towards the person who had just saved his life, he didn't show it. He wore a deep frown, and his expression was as flat as his nose. Max sensed that it was taking all his restraint not to attack him.

Instead, the Jackal turned to his men and barked an order. They quickly exited the building. There was shouting outside. It sounded like they were dispersing the Blue Command personnel outside the warehouse. While that happened, Max hurried over to Beatriz. She still crouched beneath the trestle table, clutching the switch that had engaged the lights and the cameras. He allowed himself a smile. 'You nailed it, Beatriz,' he said.

Beatriz stood slowly. 'Why are you wearing his balaclava?'

'Let's say I'm camera-shy.'

'I thought he was going to shoot you.'

'Which one, Guzman or the Jackal?'

'Both.'

'Yeah,' Max said. 'It was touch and go.'

Beatriz looked confused. She obviously didn't understand the phrase. But Max had already turned away. The Jackal was standing in front of the entrance, his weapon by his side, looking at Max with hatred. Max walked over to him, past Guzman's body.

'I should kill you now,' the Jackal said, barely moving his lips, speaking very quietly so the camera wouldn't pick him up.

'Yeah, about that,' Max said. 'Probably best you don't, unless you want to be known far and wide as a kid-killer. Play your cards right, though, and you'll be a hero of the favela. Everyone will know you were the guy who brought down Blue Command. They've seen it on telly. There's not much money in being one of the good guys, of course, but we all have to make sacrifices.'

'There will be other gangs,' the Jackal growled.

'Sure,' Max said. 'But it'll be too risky for you to start working for them, don't you think?'

The Jackal gave him a flat look. 'I'm just doing my job,' he said.

'Great. Then you've got two more tasks to do, as you're feeling so professional.' Max jabbed one thumb over his shoulder. 'Release her. Then get your guys to take us both in your armoured vehicle to Escola Rodrigues Leandro.'

The Jackal frowned. 'Why do you want to go there?'

'We're getting a lift with some friends,' Max said.

20

Escola

Abby couldn't feel the pain in her arm any more. She was so cold.

Icy cold.

Her eyes were closed. She could hear the revving of an engine and feel the warmth of someone's hand on her brow.

And voices. She could hear voices. *Abby . . . Open your eyes . . . Stay with us . . .*

Part of her wanted to obey. But it was much – much – easier to let sleep come. That way, she wouldn't be so cold any more.

The vehicle juddered. Something knocked her wound and the pain returned. She gasped.

Abby . . . Wake up . . .

The pain subsided again. The icy numbness returned. She was only half conscious now, in that pleasant shadow-world between wakefulness and sleep. Her head was a riot of images. Dead-eyed gang members in dark corners of the favela. Little Pepe, giggling in the safe house. Guzman, wild-eyed, waving his submachine gun in the air. Kissing Max.

Max.

She saw him in her mind's eye. His calm, serious face. She saw the furrow in his brow as he prepared to abseil through the roof of the warehouse. Had he glanced at her before disappearing through the roof? Or had Abby imagined that?

'Max,' she whispered.

He's going to be okay. Abby, open your eyes . . .

Her eyes flickered open. Everything was a blur. The faces of her fellow cadets came in and out of focus. She was sprawled over them, and their faces told her what bad shape she was in. She felt her eyes roll and everything went black again.

'Abby, wake up!'

Lili wanted to shake her friend back into consciousness, but she wasn't sure if it would be safe to do so. Besides, the vehicle was shaking them enough. Angel was driving like a Formula One racer, swinging around sharp corners at high speed, tyres screeching, rubber burning. Pedestrians jumped out of their way.

Lili put her hand on Abby's brow. She had never known anyone to be so cold. She was about to shout at Angel to go even faster when the Watcher hit the brakes and they came to a sudden, noisy halt. They were at the foot of a hill, outside a concrete building with big, colourful flowers painted on the side and a large sign that bore the word *Escola*.

School.

Hovering above the school was a helicopter.

'The pick-up point!' Sami exclaimed. Woody and Angel were already out of the vehicle. Angel opened a rear passenger door while Woody stood in front of the school, holding his arms in the air at eleven and one o'clock: the helicopter marshalling position, indicating that the chopper should land there. As Sami and Angel carefully lifted the unconscious Abby out of the back of the car, the chopper rose a few metres, then hovered over Woody.

Woody ran back, allowing the chopper to land. As soon as it had landed, the side door opened and Hector appeared. His face was stormier than usual as he jumped out, his hair ruffled by the downdraught. He took in the scenario with a single glance. He stepped aside to let Sami and Angel carry Abby into the chopper, then he turned to Tommy. 'You!' he roared. 'Get in!'

Tommy scurried into the helicopter as Hector turned to Lili. There was no acknowledgement that they had succeeded in their mission. Hector clearly only had one question on his mind. 'Where's Max?'

'We don't know,' Lili shouted back.

She had never seen Hector look so alarmed. As Woody hustled Pepe into the chopper, Hector clutched his hair then plunged a hand into his jacket and withdrew a handgun from his chest holster. He cocked the weapon then looked around the area as if orientating himself. It seemed to Lili as if he was prepared to take on the whole favela single-handed. She grabbed his arm. Hector's face grew even darker.

'Wait,' she shouted. 'He'll be here any minute. I promise you.'

'You said you didn't know where he was,' Hector roared back.

'I don't,' Lili shouted back. 'But I swear to you, he's on his way.'

She didn't finish. At the end of a street to their ten o'clock, a vehicle appeared. Lili recognised the BOPE's armoured car – huge, black and threatening – from earlier that night. The bumpers were high and heavy, the chassis sturdy and bulletproof. There was a tiny square windscreen at the front but otherwise it looked utterly impenetrable as it trundled towards them, its headlights burning bright.

'*Get back!*' Hector barked. Lili and Lukas stepped back beside him as Hector raised his weapon two-handed and pointed it at the armoured vehicle, which came to a halt in front of them. The air was a cacophony of machinery: the spinning rotors of the chopper and the low grind of the BOPE's armoured car. Lili's ears were numb. Unarmed, she stood her ground with Lukas while Hector kept his handgun aimed at the BOPE vehicle. The weapon was no match for the armoured vehicle. It was a symbolic gesture of defiance.

Nothing, and nobody, moved.

Then the doors of the BOPE vehicle opened. Six armed police officers, their faces covered with black balaclavas, exited. They took up firing positions on either side of the armoured vehicle and raised their assault rifles. If it came to a firefight, their firepower would completely overwhelm

Hector's handgun, but he didn't lower it. His face was stony. He didn't move.

Lili could feel the blood pulsing through her veins. She glanced sidelong at Lukas, who had sweat on his brow but who showed no sign of retreating.

Movement. A seventh BOPE officer emerged. He too wore a balaclava, but his bore a silver insignia on the front.

Lili felt bile rising in her throat. Maybe she had been mistaken. Maybe she hadn't seen what she thought she had on the TV screen.

Nobody moved. Not Hector. Not the BOPE officers. Not the Jackal.

Hector spoke. 'Get into the chopper, both of you.'

Lili and Lukas glanced at each other. They took a step back.

Then somebody else emerged from the armoured car. A girl. She had dark matted hair and grimy skin. Her eyes darted nervously from left to right and she stood by the vehicle, as though uncertain what to do next.

Then a final figure climbed out. Lili's pulse raced even faster – with relief, rather than fear.

Max moved calmly. He stopped alongside the girl and said something to her. Then he turned to the Jackal. Lili could see the hate in the Jackal's eyes through his balaclava. But the BOPE officer just nodded. He walked past his men towards Hector. Max and the girl – surely this was Beatriz – followed.

They stopped a few metres from Hector and the cadets. Hector kept his weapon trained on the Jackal. He turned to Max again. Lili was close enough to hear, over the noise of the machinery, what he said.

'Never set foot in this favela again.'

Max inclined his head. 'Next time you feel like taking money from a gang lord, or shooting a defenceless kid, remember that everybody knows who you are now.' He turned to his friends and nodded. 'Let's get out of here.'

Max led Beatriz up to the chopper and they disappeared inside. Hector still hadn't moved. The Jackal stepped up to him, seemingly unconcerned by the pistol pointed at his face.

'You call yourself a man,' he said, 'when you get children to do your dirty work for you?'

Finally Hector spoke. 'They made short work of you,' he said. 'You should learn some respect.'

The Jackal's eyes narrowed behind his balaclava. He had no response.

'Get into the chopper,' Hector told Lili and Lukas. They ran back to the helicopter. Inside, Abby lay on a stretcher. A drip had been inserted into the back of her hand and Angel was suspending a saline bag from a hook above her. Max was by her side, holding her other hand. Pepe was at the front, sitting on the floor, clasping his knees. At the back of the chopper, Tommy and Beatriz were hugging. Sami stood awkwardly by them. He looked relieved when Lili and Lukas arrived and he was able to move over and join them.

'Angel says she'll be okay,' he told his friends, pointing at Abby. He grinned. 'I'm sure I saw her perk up when Max held her hand.'

Lili looked around the dull, military interior of the helicopter. 'Yeah, well,' she said, 'it doesn't get more romantic than this.'

They watched Hector. He hadn't turned his back on the BOPE or lowered his weapon. He was walking backwards towards the chopper. When he reached it, he turned and jumped in, then slammed the door shut. 'Go!' he shouted at the flight crew. 'Get out of here, now!'

The chopper rose into the air. Lili pressed her face against the window. The BOPE were still in position down below, but the Jackal was storming back to his vehicle. Lili allowed herself a smile.

Then they rose above the rooftops of the favela and the helicopter turned. Dawn was arriving. The pink morning sun illuminated the rooftops and, in the distance, the ocean. She sensed someone standing behind her and turned to see Max.

'I saw you on TV,' she said. 'Quick thinking.'

'They killed Guzman,' Max said. He seemed haunted by the fact.

Lili looked over Max's shoulder at Abby. Her eyes were open.

'He'd have killed us, if he had the chance.' She felt her face harden. 'I'm not sorry he's dead.'

'Someone else will take his place soon enough,' Max said. 'I just hope that, without the Jackal's help, they won't get quite so powerful.' He frowned. 'Have you noticed how, whenever we get involved in a situation, people die?'

Perhaps Hector had overheard from the other side of the chopper because, as Max said this, he was there beside them. 'That's soldiering, Max,' he said. 'People die.' He glanced over at Abby. 'Our job is to make sure it's not the good guys.'

Max nodded. Lili looked around at her fellow cadets. It struck her that they looked older than they had when they first got together as a team. With a pang, she realised they would not be together for ever. The time would come when the Special Forces Cadets would be disbanded, because they wouldn't be teenagers any longer.

What then? She didn't know. But she hoped they would all manage to stay alive long enough to find out.

Something told her it wasn't very likely.

But for now, they were all okay. The chopper sped through the air, away from the dangers of the favela, towards safety.

Epilogue

They finished where they started. In the suite on the thirty-fifth floor of the Hilton Hotel. The chopper had set them down on the rooftop helipad. As the cadets disembarked along with Tommy, Beatriz, Pepe and the Watchers, Max saw medics waiting for Abby. He wanted to stay with her, but Angel gently moved him away. 'They'll patch her up,' she said. 'She'll be fine.'

He took a moment to watch the sun rising over Rio de Janeiro. High up, the cityscape was beautiful and peaceful. The sea stretched out invitingly to the horizon. Sunlight gleamed off the skyscrapers. Even the favelas were bathed in gold. Max turned his back on them, and on Abby, and followed the others down into the hotel.

Pepe's family were waiting for him in the hotel suite. The little boy's mother gathered him up in her arms and planted kisses all over his face. Pepe grimaced, but endured the attention in a way that made Max smile. Woody walked up to Pepe's father Manuel. 'He's a good kid,' he said. 'Without him, a few of us wouldn't have made it out of the favela.'

Manuel didn't seem to know what to say. He looked

proudly at his little boy as Woody gave Pepe a fist-bump. 'Keep practising those penalties,' Woody said. Pepe, even though he spoke no English, grinned as if he understood.

Tommy and Beatriz were sitting in a corner, holding hands. They looked exhausted and dirty. Tommy's face was bruised and beaten. They gazed at each other in a way that almost made Max feel embarrassed to watch. He was about to wander over to where Lukas, Lili and Sami were standing by the window, when the door slammed open and a man entered.

It was Tommy's father, Sir Alistair Sinclair. His hair was dishevelled and he had bags under his eyes. He looked frantically round the room before his gaze settled on Tommy. Max watched him carefully. He saw the ambassador's expression change from panic to relief in an instant. And then, just as quickly, his face became granite. He barged passed Hector and Angel as he strode up to his boy.

Tommy looked up. He was still holding Beatriz's hand, but the ambassador didn't acknowledge her presence. 'What the hell do you think . . .' he started to say.

But Tommy stood up. He was almost as tall as his dad. Something in his demeanour made the ambassador fall silent.

'I'm sick and tired of you telling people I'm a problem child,' he said. 'Ever since Mum died you want to control me. It ends now.'

The ambassador looked outraged.

'This is Beatriz. She lives in a favela. Get used to it, because you'll be seeing a lot more of her.'

'Don't be ridiculous, Tommy,' the ambassador said. 'You can't spend your time with a –'

'With a what?' Tommy demanded.

The ambassador waved his arms angrily. 'She's not good enough for you,' he said.

A silence descended on the room.

Max stepped forward. 'Actually,' he said, 'she's pretty much the smartest person I've ever met.'

The ambassador glanced at him. 'Who the hell even are you?' he said.

'He's –' Tommy started to say, but Hector interrupted him.

'He's one of the young people who just put their lives on the line to rescue your son,' Hector said. 'You can either talk to him and to the young lady with respect, or you can get the hell out of here.'

The ambassador flashed Hector a look then turned back to Tommy. 'We're leaving,' he said.

Tommy ran one hand through his blond hair. 'No, Dad,' he said. '*You're* leaving.'

For a moment, Max thought the ambassador might hit his son. He raised one arm and kept it in the air for a second before lowering it again. Suddenly Hector was at his shoulder. 'These kids have survived Blue Command and the BOPE. Do you really want to pick a fight with them?'

The ambassador hesitated. He looked at his son, then at the other people in the room, who were all staring at him. 'You haven't heard the last of this,' he said. He stormed towards the exit and out of the room.

Tommy looked like he might crumple. 'I didn't mean to upset him,' he said.

'He's an adult,' Hector told him. 'It's up to him whether

he gets upset or not. He might find that if he starts treating young people with a bit more respect, he'll have an easier time of it.'

'Careful, Hector,' Max said with half a smile. 'That was almost a compliment.'

'You earned it,' Hector said in a gruff voice. 'That was a long night's work.'

Hector walked over to Pepe's family and started talking to them. A hum of conversation descended on the room. Beatriz seemed to be consoling Tommy. Lukas, Lili and Sami were deep in conversation with Woody and Angel. Max stood by himself. He watched how Manuel put a proud hand on Pepe's shoulder. How Tommy covered his eyes, clearly upset at the argument with his dad.

All of a sudden, Max found himself thinking not of the favelas, or the BOPE, or Guzman, or gunfire. He wasn't even thinking about Abby. He thought about his own father, the father he'd never known. What kind of a dad would he have been? A dad like Pepe's, or a dad like Tommy's? And was it because they'd come so close to death that Max missed him now more than ever?

Hector saw him from across the room and approached. The grizzled Watcher seemed to size Max up before he spoke. 'He'd have been proud of you,' he said quietly, as though he could read Max's thoughts. 'Damn proud of you.'

Max nodded. 'I hope so,' he replied, and he walked across the room to join his friends.

Chris Ryan

Chris Ryan was born in Newcastle.

In 1984 he joined 22 SAS. After completing the year-long Alpine Guides Course, he was the troop guide for B Squadron Mountain Troop. He completed three tours with the anti-terrorist team, serving as an assaulter, sniper and finally Sniper Team Commander.

Chris was part of the SAS eight-man patrol chosen for the famous Bravo Two Zero mission during the 1991 Gulf War. He was the only member of the unit to escape from Iraq, where three of his colleagues were killed and four captured. This was the longest escape and evasion in the history of the SAS, and for this he was awarded the Military Medal. Chris wrote about his experiences in his book *The One That Got Away*, which was adapted for screen and became an immediate bestseller.

Since then he has written five other books of non-fiction, over twenty bestselling novels and three series of children's books. Chris's novels have gone on to inspire the Sky One series *Strike Back*.

In addition to his books, Chris has presented a number of very successful TV programmes including *Hunting Chris Ryan*, *How Not to Die* and *Chris Ryan's Elite Police*.

HOT KEY BOOKS

Thank you for choosing a Hot Key book.

If you want to know more about our authors
and what we publish, you can find us online.

You can start at our website

www.hotkeybooks.com

And you can also find us on:

We hope to see you soon!